VALENTINE VOWED

A Love & Lore Novella

J C Clayton

To contact Jacynta
Email: jacyntaclayton@gmail.com
Instagram: @j_c_clayton

CONTENTS

ALSO IN THIS SERIES

Easter Enchanted

Halloween Hexed

THIS STORY IS DEDICATED TO

To my husband Phill.
We've been together for twenty years now. Through so much growth and change and all the ordinary magic of building a life side by side.
You may be reading this for the first time from another country, but you are still my safe place. My steady ground. The person I want to tell first when the words finally work.
Thank you for helping me build a life where I get to write these stories.

CHAPTER 1

February 6
TRISTAN

Seraphine's voice had that smooth, endless cadence that made even our divine mission sound like the DMV's hold music. "...and if the revised clause passes the Senate, we'll need to update our contract templates before the next quarter," she said, clicking through another slide. The projector's hum blended with the rain ticking at the windows of the west conference room.

I tried to focus. Really, I did. But we'd been sitting for an hour discussing marriage legislation, and all I could think about was how ironic it was that the *Order of Lofn*—The champions of wild, forbidden love—held meetings that could put Cupid himself to sleep.

Thomas sat across the table, posture perfect, pen moving in neat lines across his notebook. He could probably recite every statute by heart. Reliable, brilliant, but if I'm honest, a little broody and taciturn. Still, he was my best friend and, lately, the only thing keeping me from drifting completely into daydreams.

Seraphine advanced another slide. "—and onto our next point of business, the Saint Valentine exhibit opens Monday. Public relations must remain pristine. No surprises. And on that note, we're still in need of a night security guard to—"

That was when the air changed.

The low hum of the projector cut out. The drizzle trickling down the windows froze, each droplet suspended like glass beads.

I glanced at Thomas who was frozen mid-blink. Seraphine, mid-gesture. The second hand on the clock stuck between a tock and a tick.

Then I felt the warmth.

A pulse of energy rolled through the room, soft but engulfing. The air shimmered near the far side of the room, and she stepped through, the wall yielding like mist around her.

The goddess, Lofn.

Copper-threaded through her blonde braids, scuffed brown leather boots molded to her calves, and a white peasant blouse embroidered with old runes that glimmered in the light was tucked into a pair of high-waisted light blue jeans. She carried the scent of pine and candle smoke and something faintly metallic —like lightning that hadn't struck yet.

"Tristan Roswell," she said, smiling. "Have you gotten more handsome since we last spoke?"

I'd been receiving visits from Lofn since I was a boy, and she always left me awestruck. I tried to stand up, to bow or kneel or something, but Lofn waved an amused hand at me, before I could pick my jaw back up from the conference table. "Don't get up. All that bowing and grovelling ruins the mood."

Her teasing cut through my awe. I laughed once, shaky. "My lady Lofn, you can't blame a man for trying to up his game in the presence of your sublime self."

A smile lifted her lips, "That flattery is why you've always been my favorite prophet".

"Something tells me you aren't here to just be flattered though..." I said. Lofn usually only visited when she had a new couple she needed me to work with, or if there was some event or political shift coming that she needed the Order to be aware of.

She stared up at Seraphine's presentation as she trailed her fingers along the back of an empty chair, the frozen world shifting faintly around her touch. "The world keeps inventing new ways to forbid love. Yet the Order is still pretending spreadsheets are holy scripture."

I swallowed a laugh.

"Even love needs auditors, hm? And yet you, my little heartkeeper, have given enough of yourself to the rules. Don't you think?"

She had asked the question so lightly, like one asks about an opinion on the weather, but something in her words made my chest tighten.

I had never thought of it as *giving myself up.* The Order had given me structure. Purpose. A place to stand.

I swallowed.

"I serve the Order," I said carefully. "And I serve

you. I've never known those things to be separate."

"The *Order*," she echoed, testing the word. "Such a serious name for a house of hearts. You serve love, Tristan. That's why I've always kept you close."

There was something different about this visit. Under her playful banter and casual perusal of the room, she seemed tense, or maybe sad. Lofn had always been playful and even flirtatious, but she was also usually far more to the point. She seemed to be procrastinating this time for some reason.

She circled behind Seraphine's motionless form, studying her as though she were a statue. "Your High Priestess does good work. Tireless, righteous. But righteousness grows brittle when it forgets pleasure."

Her gaze landed on Thomas.

He was caught halfway through turning a page, brow furrowed, the edge of his mouth soft with concentration. The expression looked almost comical with his eyes half open. Lofn's expression shifted to fondness, almost pride. "And my quiet scholar. He's carried reason like a shield for too long."

"What are you trying to tell me?"

She looked back at me, eyes bright as the copper spun through her hair. "That the ones who preach love should learn to *feel* it again. Both of you. You've given years to my cause, asking others to leap while you stand safely at the edge. That ends now."

My stomach dropped. "You want us to be married?"

"I want you to find love." She came closer, resting a warm palm briefly against my cheek. It was sometimes easy to get caught up and forget that the being before me was no mere mortal woman, but a goddess that had walked this earth for thousands of years. The sensation of her divine touch was a visceral reminder on my skin, sending shivers down my spine and gooseflesh up my arms. "When the unbound flame enters your hall, don't smother it with duty. Don't worship from afar. Take it."

The words hit harder than any prophecy she'd ever given me.

"My lady," I said slowly, trying to keep my footing, "my vows are to the Order. To you. That has always been enough."

She laughed, soft and teasing. "Oh, Tristan. You hide behind devotion the way Thomas hides behind logic. You speak of vows as if they must replace one another, when love has never worked that way."

"I'm not hiding from anything," I said, though my pulse betrayed the lie as it thudded in my throat.

She arched a brow in challenge. "Then prove it. Let yourself burn a little. Love isn't a relic in a display case. It's a living thing, and it's coming for you soon."

She turned, brushing her fingers over Thomas's still hand. "Tell him the same, when you wake."

Then she looked back at me, the warmth and wicked amusement returning to her eyes. "And Tristan? Try not to fall asleep in meetings. It's undignified for prophets."

The world snapped back with a clap of sound. The projector hummed, rain thrummed against the windows, and Seraphine's voice restarted mid-sentence.

"—help ensure the safety of the Valentine relics."

I jerked my chin up from where it had fallen against my chest, with a snort loud enough to make both of them jump.

Thomas blinked, finishing his note, then looked at me with eyebrow raised in a manner so like Lofn's it caused me to double-take.

Seraphine paused. "Everything alright Tristan?"

I cleared my throat, heat crawling up my neck. "Yes. Sorry. Long night prepping for the exhibit."

She gave me a cool, assessing glance and went back to her slides.

I avoided Thomas scalding eyes until the meeting finally ended.

When Seraphine left, shutting the door behind her, Thomas leaned back in his chair. "Lofn?"

"Yeah…." I hesitated, fingers drumming the table, wondering how best to frame what she's just shared with Thomas.

Normally, I would have told Seraphine everything the moment the vision ended. She expected it. The Order depended on it. But this time, something in me had balked. Thomas watched me, patient as ever. Waiting.

"She said something's coming," I said finally. "Someone."

"We always have someone coming. That's the

work."

"Not like this." I stopped, fingers ceasing their drumming to instead curl around the edge of the table. "She said we've been speaking about love for too long without actually living it."

That got his attention.

"She told you that?"

"She told *us* that," I corrected quietly. Specifically told me to pass it on to you too."

Thomas frowned, the crease between his brows deepening as he turned it over. "What does that even mean?"

I swallowed.

"She said we deserve to feel it for ourselves. That when 'the unbound flame enters our hall,' we're supposed to take it." I said, the words still strange in my mouth.

Silence stretched.

"Unbound flame," Thomas said at last. "Poetic." He rubbed the bridge of his nose. "Possibly dangerous."

"Yes."

"Disruptive."

"Almost certainly."

He exhaled slowly, gaze dropping to the tabletop. "And you didn't tell Seraphine."

The observation wasn't an accusation. It was a fact.

"No."

"Why?"

The answer came before I could soften it.

"Because if I follow this one, I don't know what it will

cost."

Thomas looked up then, really looked at me.

The Order had given me a place. A name. A reason to stay.

Lofn had given me purpose — but the Order had given me *belonging*.

Thomas was quiet again for a minute, leaving my knuckles white as they continued to grip the table. Then, "We'll handle it when it comes," he said. "Together."

It wasn't reassurance.

It was a promise.

I huffed out the breath I didn't realize I was holding, and felt my fingers release their grip. Instead, I picked up my notebook, and stood.

"Let's just hope," Thomas added dryly, "that whatever this unbound flame is, it has the decency to wait until after the Saint Valentine exhibit opens."

I didn't smile this time.

Somewhere deep in my chest, something had already begun to burn.

CHAPTER 2

February 6
POPPY

I sent the ball over the net fat and slow, a gift, but Ava still panicked and hacked at it. The ball veered, and her miss cast a long yellow arc against the clean white dome over Court 2.

"Stop. Breathe," I said. "You keep trying to kill it. We're not in a knife fight. Meet the ball, let it come to you. Don't attack it."

Ava blew out a frustrated sigh, sweat running along her temple. Outside, the air was ice. Inside, the dome trapped the bright winter light, and the indoor heater hummed as it pumped dispersed the heat and the scent of lemon cleaner and eucalyptus.

I fed another ball. "Keep your wrist soft and turn your hips."

She swung. Thwack. The ball cleared the net cleanly and pushed down the court landing exactly where I'd told her to aim.

Ava blinked. "I did it."

"You did it," I said, my voiced excited and

encouraging. "Again."

We did ten more. She missed two and cursed crassly under her breath each time. I liked her for that. She wasn't here to flirt or pretend. She wasn't false or pretentious like some of my other clients. She was here because she actually wanted to get better. Not just to show off her ass in a pair of new Lululemons.

At Verve Athletic & Spa, the smoothie bar might blend turmeric and ashwagandha into neon gold, but the smiles on the people here were more synthetic than the yoga mats rolled under their arms. It all looked perfect, and it paid the bills, but I never felt like I belonged. If I like you, I'll tell you straight. And if I don't, I don't whisper behind your back. But here, gossip burned more calories than Pilates.

Ava was one of the few exceptions to all this, which was why she was one of my favorite clients.

"Last five," I said. "Same swing. Trust it."

She hit all five with a perfect pop of the strings, a sound I loved. Clean. Exact. That sweet spot told the truth every time.

I jogged to the net and held up my palm. She slapped it, grinning.

"Homework," I said. "Ten minutes of shadow swings in your kitchen. Practice without a ball or even a racquet, just so your body stops fighting your brain."

"You'll be here tomorrow?" she asked, hopeful. "I have a court at nine. I thought I'd book another half hour."

"I don't have a shift tomorrow," I said. "But next week, yes. Text me and I'll squeeze you in."

Ava hesitated before slinging her bag over her shoulder.

"If you're not here tomorrow, I'll just rebook for next week. I'd rather wait for you than pick up with Brett or Alycia."

She gave a small grimace that said everything about what she really thought of Verve's other tennis staff.

"Last time I had a lesson with Alycia, she was more interested in telling me how best to pose my action shots for better TikTok thirst traps. You actually teach. And you don't pretend to be someone you're not."

I grinned in a way that I hoped let her know I agreed with her opinion of both Alycia and Brett, even if I couldn't voice it aloud like she could. Instead, I just said, "I'll look forward to seeing you next week then".

I watched as Ava slipped out through the gate. But didn't immediately move to follow her. Instead, I picked up a few balls for myself and headed back out onto the court. The dome's light caught the strings of my racquet, the court crunched under my shoes, and the serve rolled through my ribs just right. Clean. Certain. Mine.

I shot off more serves for another twenty minutes or so, before finally collecting all the loose balls and dropping them in the hopper.

I missed competing. Not enough to chase rankings again, but enough to miss the feeling of certainty. The click of strings. The way your body answered the moment before you thought too hard. Teaching gave me a piece of that, and I liked sharing my skills with people who never thought they'd feel strong. I liked that there were people, like Ava, who enjoyed finding that strength in themselves.

Ava had been my last client for the day, and I let my thoughts drift as I headed toward the staff rooms to sign out for the day. The dome door hissed open as I stepped into the corridor that connected the courts to the main building. Cool air hit me, heavy with lemon grass and whatever essential oils the spa diffused on Fridays to encourage people to buy package deals. The floor changed from court-side rubber to polished terrazzo. I pushed through the glass doors into the lounge. The space opened wide, matte white walls, soft gray couches, and a fireplace with fake logs that glowed warm for ambience. People curled on the cushions in their matching crop tops and leggings, scrolling, or posing for selfies.

The water station separated the lounge from the entrance foyer. Large condensation covered carafes full of sliced cucumber and lime, glowing under a strip light. I angled toward it, planning to fill my bottle before slipping into the staff corridor for a quick shower and heading home. The place might be pretentious, but they didn't skimp on the designer body lotions in even the staff bathrooms.

I got distracted by a patron walking through the entrance with a puppy in her tote bag, and didn't see my boss, Marla, until I nearly walked straight into her.

"There you are," she said. "We need to talk about your shift tomorrow."

"I don't have a shift tomorrow."

"You do." She clicked her tablet awake. "A founding member has requested you specifically. It's a full morning. Private court. You'll do a demo set and then social drills."

I started filling my water bottle, smiling despite her sharp pointed glare at what I was doing, since technically staff had their own water coolers out the back. "I requested tomorrow off weeks ago. You approved it."

Marla's brow pinched. "No. That was for *next* Saturday."

"It was for next Saturday," I said. "*And* this Saturday." My words were calm. But my chest wasn't. "I told you. I've got two weddings to go to. One this weekend, and one next. I asked for both Saturdays off. You said yes."

She stared at the tablet like it might confess. "Two weekends in a row is outrageous. I would never have approved that."

"You did."

Voices drifted from the lobby around us. The door swished as a pair of yoga clients slipped in to cut across to the smoothie bar. I could feel them slow, listening.

But there was no way I was going to back down. The wedding tomorrow was for my college girlfriend, Blair. Our sexual relationship hadn't lasted more than a few months, but she'd remained one of my closest friends in the years since. There was no way I wasn't going to be there for her. And next weekend was my sister, Daisy's wedding. So, no way I was going to miss that either. Was it ideal having back-to-back? No. But that's why I'd made sure to clear it with Marla weeks ago.

Marla tapped the screen. "I see a note for next Saturday. Nothing for tomorrow. We're very clear about our policies, Poppy. We can be flexible, but we need loyalty. The club has standards."

"So do I," I said. "You looked me in the eye when I asked and said, 'Of course, darling. Family first.'"
It probably wasn't my most sensible move to put on a snooty accent as I said the last part, mimicking Marla's British quip. But I could already feel that familiar pressure behind my ribs, the one that flared whenever someone decided their priorities outranked mine and expected me to be agreeable about it.

Her mouth pulled. "Please don't put words in my mouth."

"I'm not putting anything in your mouth. Just repeating what your mouth said to me."

I knew my voice was carrying. I could feel a growing spark of defiance that made me louder instead of smaller, sharper instead of conciliatory. A smarter person might've lowered their tone. I wasn't feeling particularly smart.

More people paused in the lounge and foyer, the high ceilings catching every syllable and tossing it back amplified. Even if they hadn't, my voice tends to travel when I'm annoyed.

Marla leaned closer, her smile losing its topcoat. "Lower your voice."

"Why?"

"Because you're making a scene."

"You came up to me."

"The founding member expects you," she said. "We can discuss the rest later."

I felt a switch flip in my head. I had been good here. I had been useful, taken extra shifts, covered other trainers' clients. I prided myself on being highly requested for being the kind of instructor who made people feel proud of themselves. I had swallowed the gossip and the sideways looks and the little passive aggressive comments about my fluid sexuality. I had said nothing when a client asked who I was dating and then asked again like I hadn't answered right the first time.

"I won't be here tomorrow," I said.

"You will," she said, like a mother to a child.

My laugh was sharp. "No."

Her eyes cooled. "You refuse again, and you won't be here at all."

"That's the offer?" I asked. "Perfect."

I lifted my voice now, intentionally projecting it so it carried across the growing crowd. "Attention, Verve Athletics and Spa. Since we're all about clarity and standards, let me be crystal. I, Poppy Everly, will not be here tomorrow. Or next week. Or week after that. Because I quit."

The lobby went quiet. Even the blender at the juice bar paused.

Marla took a step back as if I'd gone feral. "You're being ridiculous."

"No. I'm being honest." I pulled the embroidered

club towel off my shoulder and draped it over a nearby couch.

"You're throwing away your career," she said, voice flat with disbelief.

"I already did that when I agreed to work at this fake as fuck content creation farm posing as a wellness centre."

I slung my racquet bag over my shoulder and stormed off to the staff rooms to gather my stuff. It didn't take me long, I only kept a few things in my locker. I emptied it all into my bag: Two spare pairs of socks, a tin of grips, and a tube of sunscreen. My hands shook for exactly three seconds, then steadied before I left the lanyard with my name and access fob on the bench. I did take a second to look longingly at the showers, before muttering "fuck it" to myself and swiping a bottle of the body lotion and stuffing it into my gym bag.

Thankfully there was a back entrance off the staff rooms that slipped me out right into the carpark, so I didn't have to walk through the mess I'd just made in the foyer.

Outside the winter air slapped me. The sky was a dull pewter bruise. My breath clouded. The lot was a checkerboard of black SUVs and clean white sedans. My little green hatchback crouched in the far row under an almost bare maple. There was one orange/brown leaf clinging to the end of a branch. It rattled like a coin in a tin when the wind poked it.

I tossed my bag in the passenger seat and slid behind the wheel. The vinyl was cold through my leggings. I shut the door and the quiet wrapped around me. My hands went numb on the steering wheel. Then the adrenaline started to shake loose inside me, not fear, not yet, just shock leaving the body.

"Holy shit," I said to the empty car.

I had just quit. Loudly. In front of the blender and the eucalyptus towels and Marla's over laminated eyebrows.

I let my head tip back against the headrest and stared at the car ceiling like it might offer a map to what the fuck I was going to do now.

The smart move would have been to write a polite resignation letter, play out the job for two more weeks, network my favorite clients for new opportunities or for freelance lessons, then leave when it wouldn't scorch any earth. The smart move would have been patience.

Patience has never been my strong suit.

I wasn't panicking. At least not yet. My rent was cheap, and I could pick up something temporary until something better came along. Until then I would give all my attention to Blair this weekend, and then to my sister to help make sure both had a perfect wedding day and figure the rest out afterwards. I loved weddings. At least I loved other people's weddings. The joy, the speeches, the open bar. It was marriage I'd never been convinced I was built for.

I watched the maple's dead leaf shake on its twig until the twig finally let go. The wind carried it. It didn't fall straight down. It skated and turned and caught the air and flew crooked toward the hedges by the far curb.

I turned the engine and turned the heater on full. It coughed, then blew warm air that smelled faintly like dust. Then I pulled out, checked the rearview, and watched the glass doors of Verve Athletic & Spa disappear in my rearview mirror. The light outside went from pewter to steel. A breath of snow flirted at the edge of the sky. The road opened ahead, clean and dark.

"Something good is coming." I said it once out loud, ashamed there was still a tremor in my voice. So, I repeated it again, louder. I rolled down the window, let the cold bite my nose, and shouted the words again and again, the sound tearing out of me and vanishing into the wind. If I didn't think it was crazy, I could almost have sworn I heard laughter dancing on the wind in reply.

CHAPTER 3

February 7
TRISTAN

T he city always looked softer from a rooftop.Down on the street it was all horns and exhaust and a wind that knifed through your coat. Up here, the February air was still biting, but the noise fell away. Heaters glowed under tall mushroom-shaped lamps. Strings of warm bulbs crisscrossed overhead. The skyline rose in clean lines of glass and steel.

I stood under the arch Blair and Paige had decorated themselves. White roses, dried grasses, a few stems of dark eucalyptus. It smelled like cold air and fresh cut flowers and nerves.

"Is the mic okay?" Blair called, her voice carrying from the far side of the rooftop.

She was in a deep emerald-green suit that cut down almost to her waist with no shirt underneath. Her dark hair was slicked back and a large white pearl sitting at the hollow of her throat. Paige stood beside her in a simple satin slip dress the color of champagne, a fluffy fur wrap around her shoulders, a matching white pearl around her neck too. She was laughing at something their photographer said, but her body still seemed to be orientated towards Blair. They each orbited around the other as if connected by their own gravity. It was beautiful to watch.

I tapped the mic, "One. Two. One, Two. Sounds good to me."

Blair crossed the rooftop and pulled me into a quick hug, the kind that held a bit more than relief for a working microphone.

"Thank you for doing this."

"You'd have eloped without me." I replied.

"Probably," Paige said, joining us, her eyes bright. "But this is better."

"Much better," Blair agreed. "You make it feel real and not... I don't know. Like we stole it."

"You didn't steal anything," I said. "You claimed it."

Paige's throat worked once. She nodded and blinked hard.

I meant it, too. They weren't just words to keep my client happy. Not that I considered the couples I worked with 'clients'.

This was the part of the work the Order of Lofn did that really mattered. This moment—two women standing on a rooftop in winter air, waiting to speak vows to each other that only a few years ago were illegal to speak—this was why we worked so hard to manoeuvre politicians and policies.

It was why I stayed.

Why I believed.

And yet, even as I watched Blair's fierce grin, and Paige's soft, disbelieving joy, my thoughts kept slipping sideways, snagging on something else entirely.

When the unbound flame enters your hall...

The words pressed at the back of my mind, unwelcome and insistent. Lofn's voice had been light when she'd said it, almost amused, as if she hadn't just tilted the axis of my entire life. I'd spent years understanding love as something I guarded for others. Something I helped usher safely into the world, but then stepped away from.

The idea that I might be standing on the edge of it myself—

That it might already be moving toward us, toward *me* and Thomas—

I tightened my grip on the microphone I hadn't realized I was still holding.

The anticipation without knowing when or where it would be coming from, had been driving me nuts. I forced my attention back to the present, annoyed with myself for letting anything—even a goddess-granted prophecy—pull me away from the work in front of me.

Guests had begun to spill out from the elevator lobby and rooftop bar, wrapped in coats and scarves over dresses and suits. The DJ faded the music down to something soft and the ushers started lining people up.

Blair squeezed my arm. "Give us ten minutes to

freshen up and while everyone finds their seats, and then we're ready."

"I'll hold the fort," I said.

They disappeared inside, and I walked to the edge of the rooftop, away from the chattering crowd and looked out over the city again. My attention, however, was quickly pulled from the view again by a banging sound at a small emergency stairwell door to my left. All the guests had been directed to the main lifts, but by the knocking and if I wasn't mistaken—swearing—on the other side of the door, there was definitely at least one lost guest behind the door. I reached for the door handle and hoped it was unlocked. Thankfully it swung open in my hands and in a rush of cold air and fruity perfume, a woman fell into my arms. I got the impression she had been in the act of barging the door when I had opened it.

"Oh my God—sorry! And nice catch!"

She wore a short velvet wrap dress with long sleeves the color of ripe cherries. Her legs were toned beneath the cling of black tights, and one of her ankle boots was kicked up in the air as I held her almost parallel to the ground. Like we were mid-dip in an extravagant dance.

She shoved a lock of chestnut hair out of her face and looked around, cheeks flushed from the climb.

"Is this Blair Reese and Paige Vaughn's wedding?" she asked. "Or have I crashed something with better catering?"

Her eyes were green. Sharp and bright and they

made something in my chest jolt. It was about then I realized I had been staring and still not said a word.

"You're in the right place," I finally said.

She glanced at my arms still wrapped around her waist, and then returned her eyes to me with an eyebrow raise. "Are you gonna let me go there, Stranger?"

"Oh, of course." I righted her to her feet and my hands felt the loss of her body beneath them. I curled my fingers once, unsettled by how quickly my focus had slipped.

"Am I late?"

"No, right on time. Can I help you find a seat? Which bride are you here with?"

She snorted. "Well, I guess you can say I was with Blair. I'm her ex."

My brows went up before I could stop them. "Her ex?"

"Don't worry," she said, reading my face easily. "We're friends. Very mature. Lots of growth. Emotional evolution, blah blah. I'm on team happily-ever-after now."

We looked at each other a little longer than strangers usually did. The wind lifted the edge of her hair and brought her scent to me, summer strawberries and a hint of jasmine, and it made me want to lean in and take a deeper inhale. Sensibly, I stopped myself.

For a split second, the absurd thought crossed my mind—*what if this was who she meant?*

I dismissed the thought at once. I'd been thinking

about the prophecy too long already. I couldn't turn every moment of attraction into destiny just because Lofn's vision had unsettled me.

The DJ interrupted our moment with a call for people to move into the rows of white folding chairs.

"That's my cue," she said. "Can I save you a seat on Blair's side? Or are you here for Paige?"

"Both actually."

That eyebrow raised again, and she looked me up and down quizzically. I *could* tell her who I was, but to be honest I was enjoying her attention too much.

"Tall, dark, and mysterious I like it. I guess I'll see you round Stranger."

* * *

The ceremony went well.

As their celebrant, I spoke of how that Blair and Paige hadn't fallen in love in one grand sweep, but in a hundred quiet choices. That they simply learned each other. Learned how to stand together, how to bend together, how to make room for two hearts to beat in their own ways.

Love, I told them, wasn't about avoiding the hard things. It was about facing them side by side and saying, *We'll figure it out.*

As I spoke, my gaze drifted over the guests, more out of habit than anything—until it caught on a flash of cherry-red.

She sat in the second row, her elbows on her

knees, listening with a kind of fierce focus. When she had realized I was the one officiating, her lips had parted in a small, startled *oh*.

She didn't seem to school her reactions like most people. I saw every shift, not just at my presence officiating the wedding, but throughout the ceremony too. She softened at the vows, she blinked rapidly when emotion threatened, the little smile she gave herself as if she couldn't believe she'd teared up.

At one point she caught me watching. For a breath, neither of us looked away.

Then, finally she dropped her eyes, smiling faintly.

I gathered myself, finished the reading, and guided Blair and Paige through their vows.
Their kiss drew cheers. And as guests stood, clapping and wiping their eyes, I found myself looking once more toward the second row and toward the woman in red who was also getting to her feet, brushing at her cheeks.

Afterward, the crowd flowed toward the glass doors at the far end of the rooftop, where inside the rooftop bar, staff had set up high-top tables with black cloths and flickering candles. I signed the marriage license with Blair and Paige, then made my way inside after them, loosening my tie.

I was debating between water or wine when someone bumped my arm.

The woman from the roof stood beside me at the bar, cheeks still flushed, hair now slightly wild from the wind.

"Congratulations," she said.

"I'll pass that on to the brides," I said. "I just said some words."

"You said good words." She tipped her chin toward me. "That line about love being learned, I felt that in my spleen."

"In your spleen?"

"I don't know where feelings live," she said. "I imagine it's somewhere squishy."

The bartender leaned in. "What can I get you both?"

"Sparkling water with lime," I said, already knowing I was going to need a clear head to keep up with this little spitfire woman.

"Vodka lime and soda," she said.

"Coming right up."

She turned back to me. "So... Is this your full-time gig? Marrying lesbians on rooftops?"

"It's a good chunk of my week, yes." I laughed. "Is crashing onto rooftops your full-time gig?"

She laughed, and the sound slid under my ribs and stayed there.

I was suddenly very aware of her, the easy confidence in the way she stood, the way she met my gaze without flinching. The thought that this could be nothing more than a flirt, a drink, a night that ended with a smile and a memory, felt... possible.

So did the thought that it might be more. Could she be the woman Lofn foretold? And if she wasn't, was there any point in pursuing anything with her anyway?

And that uncertainty, that edge between appetite and fate, it made my pulse kick harder than it had any right to.

Someone called my name across the roof. Paige's brother, waving me over to where the photographer was posing the family in group shots.

"You should go sign a program for someone's grandma," she said.

"You'll still be here later?" I asked.

She shrugged one shoulder, the cherry dress shifting. "Depends how long the open bar lasts."

"I'll try to find you before it ends," I said.

"See that you do, Stranger," she replied, with a look that sent a bolt straight to my cock.

I found Blair near the cake table an hour later, her shoes already off. She glowed in a way that had nothing to do with the string lights.

"You did so good," she said, hugging me again. "People keep telling us it felt... real."

"It is real," I said. "That's the trick."

She sniffed, laughed, wiped under one eye. "Stop. I can't cry again; my makeup will mutiny."

"Consider this your last emotional hit," I said. "After this, it's all cake."

She glanced at the three-tier showpiece.

She grinned, then tilted her head. "What about you? Big plans for Valentine's?"

I sighed. "Work. We've got a Saint Valentine exhibit opening at the manor. Bones and relics and three different museums fighting over humidity levels."

"That sounds more morbid than romantic," she said.

"Don't forget stressful," I said. "We still don't have a proper night guard lined up. It's a security nightmare. The Order is twitchy. I'm pretty sure Thomas is losing sleep ranking risk factors."

"At a museum?" she asked.

"Yeah, remember the last time a religious group lent something to a progressive outfit like ours and it got defaced?" I said. "Everyone wants us to succeed as long as we don't actually do or change anything."

"So," she said. "You need someone who can handle crazy without flinching."

"Exactly," I said. "But we also need them by, like, yesterday. No one good is free on that kind of notice."

Blair's eyes shifted past my shoulder. Her face lit up.

"You might be in luck," she said, and then she was gone, weaving through the crowd.

I turned and watched her beeline for my woman in red. *My?*

She was laughing with Paige near the DJ table, shoes already off, bare black-tights feet on the cold tiles like it wasn't below 30°F outside. Blair grabbed her hand and said something. Her brows shot up and looked over at me, then back at Blair, before letting herself be dragged across the room.

My pulse picked up before they reached me.

"Tristan," Blair said, a little breathless. "Meet

my favorite mistake and best friend, Poppy Everly. Poppy, this is Tristan, who needs saving."

"From what?" Poppy asked. "Existential dread or actual danger?"

"Leaning toward option two," I said. "Nice to see you again."

"Likewise, Stranger" she said, eyes flicking over me in a quick, unapologetic assessment. "Blair says you're desperate."

"Desperate is a strong word," I said. "But in this case, it's not exactly the wrong word either."

She laughed. "Okay. Hit me. What's the problem?"

"Night security," I said. "We're hosting a Saint Valentine exhibit at the Heartguard Manor and Museum. All his scattered relics, brought together for the first time. It's a big deal. But also, a big target. We need someone on-site during off hours to keep an eye on things, coordinate with the alarm company, handle the usual 'no, you can't sneak onto the grounds after midnight' crowd."

"Spooky,"

"Do you have any security experience?" She wasn't exactly an imposing figure, her head barely reaching my chest. She was slender yet her arms had clear muscle definition, and her legs were also well-toned. And there was something in the way she held herself that told me not to underestimate her.

"Not officially," she said. "But I've done closing shifts, handled alarms, and chased more than one idiot off private property. I worked at Verve Athletic &

Spa until yesterday."

"Can anyone there vouch for you?" I asked.

"My clients can," she said. "But my former boss will probably say I'm 'difficult.' She'd be right. I don't like being treated like I'm lucky to orbit rich people. Is that going to be a problem?"

It should have been. Instead, I felt something warm uncurl in my chest.

"We're not that kind of organization."

She studied me for a moment, eyes sharp with interest. "So, what kind of organization *are* you, then? Besides the kind that marries lesbians on rooftops."

Blair made a small choking sound.

"Poppy!" Blair scolded.

"What? I don't want to end up working for the wrong business again."

I hesitated, trying to find an answer that was honest without being reckless. The Order of Lofn wasn't exactly a secret society or anything, but there was a large amount of discretion required for the way we worked. "We're an organization that protects and advocates for love. Although there's a lot more paperwork than you'd expect"

She smiled, quick and real. "And what does Cupid pay his employees these days? Would I also be doing a lot of paperwork? Is the museum haunted?"

"It's not haunted," I answered first.

"Liar," Blair said. "You told us last week the old chapel door opens on its own."

"It's a draft," I offered. "A dramatic draft."

Poppy's eyes narrowed with interest. "I can deal

with dramatic drafts."

"You'd be there from about eight in the evening until six in the morning," I said, steering us back. "You'd have access to the cameras, the patrol routes, the contact list if something goes wrong. The pay is decent, although the checks are usually signed by a 55-year-old woman named Lucinda, not Cupid."

"Is there space to move?" she asked. "Or am I chained to a monitor all night?"

"There's a patrol circuit," I said. "You can walk the grounds, check the exhibit rooms, talk to the statues if you get lonely."

"Do they talk back?" she asked.

"Only if you're polite," I said.

Blair nudged her. "You need the money, Poppy."

She sighed, then nodded. "Okay. I'm in."

I took my phone out. "If you want to come by tomorrow, I can show you the place. You can meet Thomas, see the security setup. If it feels wrong, no pressure. If it feels right..."

"I start guarding a bunch of dead saint pieces," she said. "And maybe a haunted chapel."

We traded phones and typed our numbers into each other's contacts. Her contact popped up in my list: **Poppy Everly** 🌶. She'd added the chili pepper herself. My chest tightened with a ridiculous amount of joy at that small, stupid icon.

"I'll text you the address," I said. "Come around two? It'll give us time before the evening rotation."

"Two works," she said. "I'll bring coffee. You look like a cold brew kinda guy."

"That's unfairly accurate," I said.

Blair looped an arm around both of us, tipsy and happy. "Look at me," she said. "Matchmaking on my wedding day."

"Tomorrow at two, then," Poppy said disengaging from the hug, with a soft look at Blair.

I watched her walk away, hips swinging, laughing at something Paige said as she met her on the dance floor.

The music swelled. Someone popped another bottle of champagne, and the city lights pressed close, a thousand small suns against the dark.

CHAPTER 4

February 8
POPPY

The driveway went on longer than I expected. The kind of slow reveal that made you sit forward and lean over the steering wheel to see the next inch of it a microsecond sooner than if you sat back in your chair.

And when I finally reached the end, I was rewarded with Heartguard Manor and Museum, all stone and wide windows and winter-bare trees standing sentinel in neat, uniformly spaced lines. The building had presence. Weight. The kind that made you feel like maybe you should lower your voice when you stepped out of the car.

I paused long enough to take it in. The grounds were immaculate without being over the top. Gravel crunched under my boots. Frost still clung to the shaded edges of the lawn. And off to the side, half-hidden by a stand of trees, was a tennis court.

I smiled without meaning to.

Okay, universe. I see you.

I parked my car in the lot and followed the path up to the front doors. Inside, the manor was warmer than I expected. Not just temperature-wise. Lived-in warm. A rack by the door with scarves and coats slung over it, a fresh purple, yellow and white flower bouquet on a side table. Somewhere deeper in the building, music played low and familiar. Florence and the Machine, I thought.

I liked it immediately.

The foyer opened into a series of gallery rooms, sunlight pouring in through tall windows and catching on glass cases and polished wood. A couple stood near the coat rack studying a brochure, whispering over a map of the permanent collection. Somewhere deeper in the building, a child's voice echoed before being quickly hushed.

I wandered through to the rooms that adjoined the foyer, staring in wonder at the Norse relics lining the walls. There were carved figures, and textiles that looked like they'd survived more winters than I could imagine. But I couldn't see an information desk or reception to check-in for my interview or announce myself in any official way.

Tristan's directions hadn't helped:

Come in the front, go via the East gallery, until you see the sign for the currently closed Saint Valentine exhibit and I'll find you.

Helpful.

Not!

I hate when people give cardinal directions. Who can tell East from West off the top of their heads?

Or am I just missing that internal compass gene? Do they just mean left and right? But then why wouldn't he just say, 'turn right?'

Rather than reach for my phone to open a compass app, I just committed and took the passage to the right.

I stepped through a wide stone archway and knew immediately I was in the right place.

If the red velvet draping curtains and cordoned of rope didn't give it away, then the easel holding up a sign that said: *Closed for installation. Opens Monday 6th February* certainly did.

I didn't see Tristan anywhere though.

I looked around quickly and saw the only other visitor in the room was an elderly man leaning close to a glass case, squinting at a plaque. He didn't seem to be paying me any mind. So, figuring I was about to be trusted as a security guard anyway, I stepped over the rope, and ducked into the next room.

The space beyond was draped in more red velvet, interspersed with baroque gold frames depicting painting after painting of cherubs. Plump little figures frozen mid-flight, arrows poised, wings blurred in oil and age. The deeper I moved into the room though, the more the sweetness gave way to weight.

The walls were crowded with paintings, some lush and theatrical, others darker and older. Saints in heavy robes. Couples standing stiffly side by side, hands barely touching, faces solemn as vows were exchanged in candlelit chapels that looked nothing like greeting cards. I tamped down my instinctual cynicism to anything relating to this holiday. This exhibit had nothing of the usual chocolate hearts and diamond ads pretending love was something you could buy if you spent enough money.

I stepped further into the room, meandering through glass cases that held rings dulled by centuries. Scraps of parchment. Objects that had once been held, worn, hidden.

And then the bones.

Saint Valentine's bones according to the plaque.

Had we built an entire industry all on this guy's bones?

I leaned closer to read the larger description plaques. It described secret ceremonies and forbidden unions, and marriages performed in defiance of law and empire. Something in my chest shifted.

"Read anything good?" a voice said behind me.

I turned. Tristan stood a few feet away, hands tucked into the pockets of a pair of black jeans. His mouth curved in a smile that felt familiar already. He looked different out of the suit he'd worn at Blair's wedding. Still handsome, obviously. Today he'd pushed the sleeves of his sweater up to his forearms, and for the first time I saw that he had tattoos—dark lines curling over muscle, that I also wanted to lean closer and inspect. His dark blonde hair was pulled back loosely, a small piece loose by his jaw.

Damn he was hot. Why is it my luck to be so sexually attracted to my boss when I believe so strongly in not shitting where you eat.

Maybe I didn't need to take this job?

Stop, I do need this. And I need to respond with something professional instead of standing here staring.

"I was just reading," I said. Real intellectual in action there. He was polite enough to move on with no more than a small smile at my expense.

"Welcome to Heartguard Manor."

"Thanks for having me," I said.

He gestured for me to follow him, and as we walked, he talked. About the museum and the larger manor it was a part of. He finally told me more about the organization he worked for. The Order of Lofn, and how they ran the whole thing. Along with all the other work they did helping change the laws around forbidden marriages. His voice shifted when he spoke about it. Not the same playful banter we'd shared at the wedding. More focused. Proud, even.

It surprised me a little.

He didn't exactly look like someone who spent his days indoors cataloguing relics and scrutinising policy documents. He looked like a guy who might be more at home on a beach in California, salt washed through his hair as he carried a surfboard under his arm.

Instead, he spoke about the history of each relic and tapestry with such passion and animation it left me captivated.

"And this," he said, slowing as we reached a smaller display tucked between two larger rooms, "is one of our stranger pieces."

The box sat on a pedestal, unassuming at first glance. Wood darkened with age. Carved with intricate patterns that made my fingers itch just looking at them. A small plaque read:

Lofn's Wedding Game. Do Not Touch.

I leaned in. "What's the game?" I asked.

Tristan hesitated. Just a beat. "No one knows. It's never been opened."

That did it.

A hum started under my skin, low and insistent. A visceral thrill in the deep nerves of my fingers. It was a feeling I'd never felt anywhere else but on a tennis court. The moment before a serve when everything narrowed and sharpened, and the world waited for you to move.

"I could open it," I declared, surprising even myself at the confidence in my voice.

He laughed. "Everyone says that."

"I'm not everyone."

The words came out too fast. Too sure.

I frowned at myself, because rationally, this was ridiculous. The box was old. Ancient, probably. Why did I think I could solve it, surely thousands had tried before it became a museum piece.

Yeah, I liked puzzles. I always have. Logic games, strategy, patterns. I trusted my hands and my instincts. But this wasn't that. This wasn't a Sunday crossword or a locked room escape game.

And still.

The box seemed to lean toward me. Or maybe I leaned toward it. I couldn't tell where the wanting started. Tristan's eyes flicked to my hands. Back to my face. His expression shifted, something cautious threading through the warmth.

"No," he said, firmer this time. "It's not a toy."

"I know," I said quickly. "I wouldn't— I mean, I wouldn't force anything. I just want to see how it moves."

I reached out without fully meaning to. His hand closed around my wrist and the contact stopped me cold.

His palm was warm, solid, and deliciously firm. The hum under my skin jumped, sharp and sudden, like static. My breath caught, and judging by the way his fingers tightened and his eyes widened for half a second, so did his.

We both looked down at where we touched. Then back at each other. Then slowly, he released me.

"I shouldn't," he said, more to himself than to me.

"I won't break it," I promised. I didn't know why I was so sure. I just was.

He studied my face, searching for something. Whatever he found there made him exhale.

"Be careful," he said.

I reached out. The wood was warm under my fingers. Like it had been sitting in the sun. despite no nearby windows. The carvings shifted under my touch, pieces sliding, clicking into place with satisfying precision. I twisted one piece. Pressed another. The box resisted, then yielded, like it had been waiting.

"What the FUCK?!" The voice was deep and loud. Very loud.

I looked up to see a man striding toward us, jaw set, eyes locked on my hands like they were holding a grenade. Yet even though my eyes were raised to watch the man almost running towards us, my hands continued to move around the slots and latches of the box.

"Step away from that," he demanded.

Something about him hit me square in the chest. Tall. Broad. Beard trimmed close. His hair was tied in a knot on the back of his head, with the sides shaved close. He looked like a viking right out of the past come to claim the old artifacts the museum held. The only thing breaking the illusion was the modern white buttoned shirt and pants he wore. And was that a pair of white gloves?

"Thomas," Tristan stepped in front of me and tried to sooth the charging beast. "She's—"

"Touching a sacred artifact," Thomas snapped. "Which is explicitly forbidden."

"I'm sorry," I said, though my hands still hadn't stopped. "I—"

When the man—Thomas was what Tristan had called him—had reached the two of us, he extended out his gloved hands to try and snatch the box from me.

Tristan placed a hand on Thomas's arm. "I said she could try."

Thomas's eyes flicked to Tristan. Then back to me. Something unreadable passed through them.

Then final piece clicked into place.

The sound was small. Satisfying. Final. I looked down at the box, the lid already popped open on its own. Inside, nestled on a scrap of aged-yellow silk, were three rings.

Simple bands. Bronze, warm-toned, almost rosy under the gallery lights.

They weren't ornate. They weren't jeweled. But they were clearly very old.

Tristan and Thomas beside me were also looking in at the box's contents, their confrontation forgotten.

My breath slowed. The room seemed to draw closer, the edges of it softening as I leaned in. One of the rings caught the light as I shifted. The metal glinted, and something in my chest answered it.

I reached in.

I didn't think about it. Didn't weigh the decision. My fingers closed around the band like they'd been shaped for it, the metal warm against my skin. I was dimly aware of movement beside me, of the others doing the same, but my focus tunneled until there was only the ring in my hand.

I set the box back on the pedestal without looking away.

The electric lights overhead reflected off the surface, which I could see now was hand-engraved with three symbols. I wasn't a big jewellery girlie. I had my ears pierced, but rings and necklaces had only got in the way when I trained. But there was something alluring about this ring. Something that called to me and whispered for me to put it on.

The rational part of my brain was warning me that listening to strange whisperings was probably not a good idea. But the more chaotic, rebellious part of me pointed out that there was little difference between listening to this rational voice and listening to the voice that wanted me to put on such an intriguing ring.

Such a simple pretty ring.

I slid it onto my finger.

For half a heartbeat, nothing happened.

Then light detonated. It burst from the ring I held, and from the other two as well. White and searing. Heat tore up my arm, slammed into my chest. Pain followed, sharp and overwhelming, stealing the air from my lungs.

I screamed.

I heard others screaming too.

The world collapsed into fire and sound and the violent rush of my own heartbeat. And then everything went dark.

CHAPTER 5

February 8
TRISTAN

The gallery ceiling swam above me, all pale plaster and beams that looked too calm for what had just happened. My limbs felt heavy, like I'd been dropped from a height and hadn't finished landing.

Poppy lay a few feet away, on her side, one hand curled near her head. The hair from her ponytail had flipped across her face. Thomas was sprawled on his back near the pedestal, from here I couldn't tell if either of them were breathing.

My pulse kicked.

I pushed up on my elbows, wincing as my head throbbed. "Poppy?" My voice came out rough. "Thomas?"

Neither moved. Panic skittered under my ribs.

"They won't answer."

Slowly, I sat up.

Lofn sat smiling at me from the top of the pedestal where Poppy had set the box. One leg crossed over the other, boot toe swinging like she had all the time in the world. The little puzzle box rested in her hand as if it were nothing more than a baseball. Her copper-threaded braids caught the gallery light and threw it back in warm flashes.

I let out a shaky breath. "This is a vision."

"It is," she said. "And you are awake enough to listen. Good."

I glanced back at Poppy and Thomas. They were still. Too still. "Are they..."

"Alive," Lofn said, as if she'd read the thought right off my face. "Stunned. Humans are so dramatic when magic touches them."

"I'm human," I muttered.

"Only partly," she said, and her eyes crinkled with something fond. "Oracles have always been... in-between."

I hated how true that landed.

My gaze dropped to the box in her hands. "You did this."

"I made the game," she corrected, tapping the lid with one fingernail. "It has sat unopened for a long time. Waiting for hands that wouldn't flinch. Waiting for a mind that likes patterns more than permission."

Her eyes flicked toward Poppy's unconscious form, and her grin grew wider.

"You like her," I said before I could stop myself.

Lofn's smile widened. "I do."

My throat went tight. "Is she... the unbound flame you told me about?"

Lofn tilted her head, considering me. She leaned

forward, elbows on her knees, the box balanced loosely in one hand. Her presence filled the room without any effort.

"You and Thomas have served," she continued, voice warm but edged with iron. "You have done your work. You have carried other people's vows like lanterns through dark places. You have stood witness and sworn yourself to this cause so much you forgot you had bodies of your own."

Heat crept up my neck. "My purpose is the Order."

"No," she said, gently and final. "Your purpose is not to be useful. Your purpose is to be whole."

The words punched a soft bruise into something I had always tried to keep locked down.

I swallowed. "Thomas won't see it that way."

Lofn's gaze slid toward Thomas. There was a quiet fondness there, like she'd been watching him for a long time. "Thomas has spent years building walls and calling it wisdom. He will rage. And then he will read until he finds the answer because that is how he loves. Through effort. Through certainty. Through control."

She lifted the box higher, letting the gallery light play over its carvings. "Now, speaking of reading. Will you please tell him: Third shelf from the bottom. The left-hand side. Red spine."

I blinked. "That's it?"

"That's it," she said brightly. "The game isn't fun until everyone knows the rules."

She said it with mock severity, but Tristan could

see the joy twinkling in her eyes. "Oh, and Tristan?"

"Yeah?"

Her eyes flicked towards Poppy. "You might want to keep her close."

The words slid into my bones, warm and strange. I opened my mouth to ask what she meant, but Lofn slipped from the pedestal like one slipping down a playground slide and disappeared into the ether.

The gallery snapped.

Sound crashed back in. The distant music resumed, Florence's voice pouring into the air like nothing had happened. I was on my back again, looking up at the ceiling. My head spun as I sat up and looked toward the pedestal. The puzzle box sat where Poppy had left it, closed and innocent.

Thomas groaned.

Poppy shifted and sucked in a sharp breath, eyes flying open. She blinked fast, then pushed herself up on one elbow.

"Oh my God," she rasped. "Did anyone else just get hit by a star?"

Thomas sat up in one rough motion, hand going to his head. His eyes found the pedestal, the box, the ring on his finger, and then Poppy. His expression hardened.

"What," he said, voice clipped, "did you do?"

Poppy's mouth opened, then closed. She looked at him, at the way his whole body seemed coiled, angry and ready. For the first time since I'd met her, her confidence faltered.

"I didn't do anything on purpose," she said. "I opened the box, yeah. But you were there. You both were. You put the rings on too."

Thomas's gaze snapped to my hand, then his own. The bronze band that sat on his finger looked the same as mine, beaten bronze etched with Norse runes. Unlike me, Thomas might actually know what they mean. His jaw flexed once.

"This wouldn't have happened if you hadn't opened the box first," he said to Poppy.

Poppy swallowed. "I'm sorry. Okay? Really, I am. It was like it pulled me to it, like I had no choice. I know that's not enough. But I am sorry."

I believed her. Because I remembered the pull. The way my hand had moved without argument. The way my body had answered the ring's call.

"I felt it too," I said quietly, watching Thomas. "The draw. We all did."

Thomas's eyes cut to mine. There was accusation in them, and something else. A warning. A promise that we would talk about this later.

Then he looked back at Poppy and took a slow breath through his nose, like he was trying to swallow down his temper.

"We need to remove them. Put them back as they were," he said.

Poppy's shoulders loosened a fraction, relief flickering across her face. She pushed to her feet. "Yes. Great. Of course." Once on her feet she moved back toward the pedestal as if to return the ring but paused. She turned back still tugging on her finger, her face pinching with the effort.

Thomas grabbed his own hand and twisted at the ring—Nothing.

His jaw tightened. He tried again, bracing his finger and pulling harder this time. The ring didn't shift.

I looked down at my own hand.

The bronze band sat warm against my skin, the runes catching the light as I turned it. I slid my thumb beneath it and pulled.

It didn't move.

"Okay," Poppy said, looking at me. "That's... not encouraging."

She tried again, twisting, pulling, even giving it a sharp yank like she might surprise it into cooperation.

Nothing.

The three of us looked at each other. Thomas exhaled slowly through his nose, his anger not as tamped down as I thought.

Poppy looked around the gallery, eyes darting like she was scanning for exits, for security cameras, for someone to tell her this was a prank. "Okay. We can figure it out. This place has a bathroom, right? I can get soap. Maybe lotion. I have some in my car."

She turned and started walking toward the archway.

She made it maybe six feet. Then she folded.

In the same second, a sharp, vicious pressure slammed into my own chest, as if a fist had reached beneath my ribs and squeezed everything squishy inside them. My vision blurred at the edges.

Thomas also made a sound between a grunt and a curse and staggered.

Poppy gasped, clutching at the air like she could pull oxygen back into her lungs.

My body moved before my mind caught up. I stumbled forward, hand outstretched.

Keep her close.

Lofn's words echoed in my mind.

I stepped towards Poppy, my feet feeling like I was traipsing through cement while the pain still clutched at my chest. But after two steps, the pain seemed to lesson, by the fourth step the pain had eased considerably. But still I continued until I was able to grab Poppy by the upper arm and haul her toward me. I pulled her in until she was close enough that I could feel her breath against my chest. The pain completely disappeared in the same instant, retreating like a wave.

Poppy blinked up at me, stunned.

"What the hell?" Thomas's voice was gruffer than normal and felt closer too. I turned to see he had also been stepping towards the archway and Poppy. His face was tight as his stormy eyes met mine.

We stood there in a tense cluster, close enough that I could smell Poppy's perfume, strawberry and jasmine. Close enough that my pulse did strange things that had nothing to do with pain.

Poppy looked between us; eyes wide. "Okay. That wasn't fun."

Thomas stretched slowly, testing his shoulders

as if he expected pain to come back for revenge. "Do it again," he said, voice flat.

Poppy stared. "Do what again?"

"Move away," Thomas said.

Poppy's expression went tight. "No offense, Viking, but I just got stabbed by invisible lightning."

"It's the only way to understand it," Thomas replied.

I kept my hand on Poppy's arm. "We can all do it," I said. "Carefully, step by step."

Poppy let out a breath, then nodded once. "Fine. But if I die, I'm haunting both of you."

We took our places in a small circle, then each stepped back one foot.

Nothing.

Another. Nothing again.

On the third the pain flickered, a warning spark under my skin.

By the fourth step, we were all wincing but pushed on one more.

This time it hit harder. Enough to make my lungs clamp making it hard to breath.

Thomas swore under his breath, then grunted out, "Enough."

We each stepped back toward each other and into the circle like some sort of fucked up Hokey Pokey. The pain eased as quickly as it came.

Poppy pressed a hand to her sternum, breathing hard. "Let's not test it again please."

Thomas's eyes were distant now, mind already shifting into problem-solving. "A radius," he said. "We have a radius."

"How big?" Poppy asked.

Thomas measured the space with his gaze, then nodded toward the floor tiles. "Six feet. Maybe seven. Beyond that, it seems the pain escalates."

"So, we're what?... Tethered?" Poppy asked, voice dropping.

She seemed to accept the supernatural weirdly well.

Thomas looked at the rings again, then turned toward the staircase that led to his library. His shoulders squared, anger turning into focus. This was his element. His safe place.

"I think I've read about this," he said, and Poppy blinked.

"You have?" I asked. It was certainly all news to me.

"Bring the box." And on that note, he turned on his heel and began to march toward the library. After two steps I heard him wince and slow his pace. I grabbed the box from the pedestal and Poppy and I followed him to the staircase.

In his library, Thomas stood in front of the meticulously ordered shelves, scanning.

"Third shelf," I said quietly. "From the bottom. Left-hand side. Red spine."

Thomas's head snapped toward me. His eyes narrowed. "How do you know that."

I held his stare. "Just trust me."

He seemed to understand when I flicked my

eyes up and back and didn't say anything further. Just exhaled, sharp, and pulled the book free.

The cover creaked when he opened it, paper thick and old. Thomas flipped through with fast precision, until he seemed. To find the page he was looking for.

His eyes moved across the text, and something in his face shifted.

"This is Lofn's handfasting, or wedding game," he said finally, voice low.

Poppy's eyebrows shot up. "Are you telling me we're married now?"

Thomas kept reading. "Not exactly. It's a binding. A test. Intended to come before a bigger commitment."

Poppy crossed her arms, the movement hampered by how close she had to stand. "How much of a bigger commitment can there be than being stuck at the hip?"

Thomas ignored her and kept going. "There's a release. But it requires three rejection rites."

My stomach tightened. "Rejection?" I repeated.

Thomas nodded once, grim. "You must verbally reject each other under specific conditions."

Poppy's mouth went a little dry. "Reject each other as in…?"

Thomas's gaze flicked to her. "You speak the rejection spell. Out loud. Together. Three times."

Poppy swallowed. Again, weirdly ok and accepting of it all. I kept waiting for her to argue or deny the possibility of it all. But she just seemed to be going with everything like it all made perfect sense that a set of magic rings could bind three people in a magical marriage. I barely believed it and I'd been living with the supernatural for the last seventeen years.

Thomas went back to the book, "The first must be spoken under the first rays of dawn. The second amidst the lightening of a storm. The third under the dark eye of the new moon."

I frowned. "And the next new moon is…"

Thomas's eyes met mine. "Valentine's Day."

The word sat in the air.

Poppy stared at him. "You're kidding."

"I am not," Thomas said.

Poppy let out a sound that might have been a laugh if it didn't have panic hiding underneath it. "So, we have a week to do three rejection rituals, while wearing cursed rings that will barely let us walk to the bathroom alone."

Thomas turned a page. "Or we could wait until the next full moon next month. To be honest it's the lightning storm that's going to be the difficult one to predict."

Poppy looked at me like I might have a better answer. I didn't.

Because underneath the shock, something else stirred in me. Wonder. The same feeling I got when a vision landed and my whole body knew it mattered before my mind could explain why.

I looked at my ring again. Lofn's game. Her promise.

Thomas closed the book with a decisive snap, his gaze cutting to Poppy again. "You will need to stay here."

Poppy blinked. "Here as in... move into the manor?"

"Yes," Thomas said, as if it was the most obvious thing in the world. "As I just explained, we cannot be separated."

Poppy stared at him. Then at me. Then at the invisible space around us like she was trying to find the edges of a trap.

CHAPTER 6

February 8
POPPY

I f you'd asked me that morning where I thought I'd be sleeping that night, it might have taken me a hundred years before the answer of 'in a historic manor, magically tied to the hip with two incredibly hot guys I'd met less than twenty-four hours ago' ever occurred to me.

Life, apparently, had other plans.

The drive back to my apartment was silent.

Not the comfortable kind. The kind where everyone was drowning in their own thoughts, and no one knew how to be the first to surface.

Thomas drove. Tristan sat in the passenger seat. Meanwhile, I was in the back, staring out the window at the blur of winter trees and wondering how the hell I'd gone from quitting my job in a blaze of righteous fury to... this.

When we got to my apartment, it felt smaller than it had that morning. Although that could have just been the two six-foot-something men following me around through it that made it feel cramped. The place wasn't messy, exactly. But it wasn't overly curated either. Mismatched furniture. A half-folded load of laundry abandoned on the couch. A stack of mail I'd been meaning to sort for weeks.

"Sorry for the mess," I said. "I wasn't planning on company."

"It's fine," Tristan said quickly. "It's... very you."

I snorted. "You've known me for less than a day."

"Still," he said, smiling.

I grabbed an overnight bag from the closet and started tossing things in without much thought. Clothes. Toiletries. Phone charger. All the while, Thomas and Tristan were never more than two steps from my side. When I passed the shelf by the window lined with puzzles I felt Thomas's gaze there, sharp and assessing. There were wooden ones, metal ones, abstract shapes that twisted and folded and locked in ways that made my fingers itch just looking at them. Some solved. Some half-solved. One I'd been stuck on for months.

"You like puzzles," he stated. He didn't say it like a question, but I answered him anyway, just to keep some sort of conversation rolling.

"Yeah," I said. "Apparently a little too much."

He didn't smile. But something in his expression eased, just a fraction. But there was no further small talk either. We didn't linger long after that.

Back at the manor, the guys showed me the

living quarters. The shift from downstairs museum to upstairs living space was immediate. The grand, echoing galleries gave way to clean lines, soft lighting and modern art on the walls. A large abstract piece in reds and golds caught my eye, and I stopped short.

"Is that a—"

"Doron Langberg?" Tristan asked. "Yeah."

I felt something loosen in my chest. "I love their work."

Tristan glanced at me, pleased, I think. Then continued to show me around.

The living suite was communal but intentional. A kitchen that looked well-used. A couch that had looked like you could sink into it and never want to get up. Two doors off the main space, each leading to private bedrooms.

"So, how is this going to work" I asked, gesturing to the two bedrooms.

Before either of them could respond, a woman stepped into the room.

This must be Seraphine. Tristan had told me about her before the whole ring, box, game thing had happened.

She was probably only a few years older than Thomas and Tristan, and composed in a way that made my spine straighten without permission. Dark hair pulled back. Expression smooth and unreadable. She took in the scene in one glance: the rings, the proximity, me.

"This," she said calmly, "is inconvenient."

Thomas stiffened. Tristan opened his mouth.

"I know," I said, too fast. "I'm really sorry. I didn't mean—"

Seraphine held up a hand. Not unkindly. Efficiently. "Intent is irrelevant. The consequences are not."

Her gaze shifted to Tristan. "You have two meetings this week."

"Yes," he said. "One I can reschedule. The other I'd like to keep if we can make it work."

"Do what you can," she directed before turning to Thomas, "The dignitaries arrive in four days. Have all the arrangements been made for their arrival?"

"Yes." He responded simply.

"Good, Lofn game or not, this exhibit must go off without any further *complications*." The last word I detected a slight curl of her lip as she directed it at me.

I swallowed. Complication. That's what I was. A walking, breathing liability.

"I can help," I said. "With anything. Monitoring cameras. Staying up. I don't need to sleep much."

Seraphine's eyes flicked back to me. Cool. Measuring. "We'll see."

That was worse than no.

She left without another word.

The silence she left behind was heavy.

"I'm sorry," I said again, quieter this time, directing my apology to both men, but only Tristan met my eyes. "I know I've fucked a lot up for you."

He shook his head. "*You* didn't fuck it up. We *all* fucked it up. There's a ring on each of our fingers too."

Thomas didn't contradict him and that felt like

a small mercy.

By the time we reached the bedroom on the right, I'd already lost count of how many times I'd almost tripped over one of them.

They were always *there*. Two steps behind me. Two steps beside me. Every turn I made echoed with the presence of someone else's body. Doorways had become the scene from one of those old black and white slapstick comedy shows like, I Love Lucy. All three of us each trying to stay close, while managing two broad shouldered men through the narrow openings.

But when it came to the bathroom, I stopped short in the doorway and spun around.

Both of them nearly collided with me.

"Whoa," I said, hands lifting instinctively. My palms hit their chests. Hard. Solid. An warm through their shirts. I felt the impact all the way up my arms, felt the way both of their bodies reacted to it, muscle tightening under my hands. For half a second, none of us breathed.

Then I dropped my hands like I'd touched a live wire.

"No," I said. "Absolutely not."

Tristan blinked. "What?"

"You are not coming in here with me."

"We can't—" Thomas started.

"I know," I snapped. "Radius. Rings. Ancient goddess nonsense. I get it. But I am not peeing with an audience."

I glanced over my shoulder into the bathroom.

It was small. Clean. One sink. One shower. One toilet tucked into the corner. I eyeballed the distances and did the math fast.

"If you both stand right here at the door," I said, pointing to the hallway just outside the door, "the *closed* door," I stressed, "We should be still close enough that I can have at least a moment of peace to myself. Brush my teeth, maybe even shower. Then, I'm sure you both wouldn't mind some privacy too, so I'll come out and we can swap."

Thomas hesitated, jaw tight, then nodded once. "Fine."

I shut the door and leaned my forehead against the wood, breathing out hard.

This was not the romantic magic my sisters had gotten.

Daisy had broken a curse literally just with magic chocolate Easter egg. Iris had played music through the veil and pulled a man back from death. How was it when they got wrapped up in supernatural curses and hexes, they got chocolate and pumpkin patches, yet I got the kind that punished me for wanting to pee alone?

Figures.

I showered quickly, hyper-aware of the faint pressure in my chest the entire time, like my body was keeping score of every inch I pushed the radius. When I'd turned the water off and wrapped tightly in a towel, I waited a beat before opening the door.

Tristan and Thomas were right there. Judging by the deep furrows between Thomas's eyebrows and the way Tristan was rubbing at his chest, the experience had been barely tolerable for them too. But despite the pain, I did feel better after a shower and a few minutes to myself.

"Are you ok?" Tristan asked softly.

"Yeah," I said. "It's just... a lot."

His gaze flicked down at my towel then away immediately, respectful, but not before I saw the awareness there. The interest. The same thing coiling low in my stomach whether I wanted it or not.

"I forgot to grab my pyjamas." They followed me to my bag, then retook their places as sentinel by the door as I changed. I slipped into a pair of flannel pants and a black tank top before stepping back out. "Ok, who's next?"

Tristan and I waited while Thomas took his turn. He told me a bit more about the Order and the weddings he'd officiated to keep ourselves distracted from the tightness in our chests as Thomas showered. When the door finally opened, Thomas emerged with his hair damp, a clean shirt clinging slightly to his still damp shoulders. He looked uncomfortable. But he took up Tristan's post without a word. Tristan shot me a quick wink then stepped into the bathroom.

"Sooo..." I started not sure how to start a conversation with this brooding viking of a man. "Tristan says your family has been part of the Order for generations?"

"Yes."

"And that you helped lobby for the equal right of same-sex marriage in countries around the world?"

"Yes."

By this point I could tell it was going to be a fight to get more than single syllable answers out of him."

"Aaaannnd that you have an irrational and deep-seated fear of chihuahuas."

"What! I am not scared of chihuahuas. Of all the ridiculous—" He stopped when I burst into laughter, literally folding at the hip belly chortling at the flabbergasted look cracking that surly veneer of his face.

I was still snickering when Tristan joined us again. He was running a towel through his hair and was wearing just a pair of low-slung grey sweatpants. His shirtless, chiselled, tattoo-adorned, still glistening wet, muscular chest and stomach on full delicious display.

Thomas cleared his throat. "We should sleep. We need to be up before dawn."

The first rejection ritual. Of course.

The bedroom was twice the size of mine, dominated by a massive four-poster king bed that harkened more to the antique heritage of this manor. It was dark wood with heavy carved lines, and textured black bedding.

Despite its size my chest still tightened at the thought of sharing a bed with these two.

"We're adults," Thomas said, already practical. "This is the only arrangement that makes sense."

Tristan nodded easily. "I'll take the middle."

Thomas took the right, facing the door, leaving me to climb in last, taking the side by the window.

The mattress dipped under our combined weight; the space immediately warmer, fuller. Tristan's body pressed closely mine, not quite touching but radiating heat down my back. I could also hear Thomas's slow steady breaths from the other side, not sure if he was doing some sort of calming exercise or had just fallen asleep the second his head it the pillow.

I lay there, staring at the dark glass, acutely aware of every breath, every shift, every inch of space I no longer controlled. This was temporary. It had to be.

We would break this thing. I would get my life back. I would not let some ancient vow decide how close I stood to anyone.

But as sleep crept in, my body betrayed my desire for space and freedom, softening toward Tristan's heat, and finding the ebb and flow of both the men's breaths soothing.

My body was clearly very comfortable here already.

And that scared me more than the pain ever could.

CHAPTER 7

February 9
TRISTAN

I woke before the alarm. That wasn't unusual. What was unusual was the weight pressed into me. Poppy.

Her back was flush to my chest, her ass nestled perfectly against my groin, warm and solid and completely unaware of the trouble it was causing. My arm was curved around her waist, hand splayed over the soft dip just above her hip, fingers relaxed like they belonged there.

They did not.

My body, however, strongly disagreed.

I lay very still, staring at the back of her head trying to will my erection away. But the sleep-warm smell of her skin invading my senses only made it worse. She shifted in her sleep, a small, unconscious wiggle, pressing back into me like she was testing the shape of me.

I sucked in a breath through my teeth.

Thomas was at my back, solid and unmoving,

the heat of him a steady line of awareness that I tried to concentrate on instead. But Poppy stirred again. Her head tipped back slightly, the crown brushing my jaw, my hand clenching the soft fabric of her tank top over her belly, fighting the urge to make contact with the soft skin beneath.

I leaned in, mouth close to her ear, voice low and rough with sleep and restraint.

"If you keep wriggling like that," I murmured, "you're going to make me stop caring that we're not alone."

Her eyes fluttered open.

For one dangerous second, there was a spark there. Something bright and wicked and curious.

Her lips curved.

Then Thomas's alarm went off.

The sound was sharp and merciless, slicing straight through the moment. Poppy jolted forward, color flooding her cheeks as awareness crashed in.

I exhaled slowly, letting my forehead rest briefly against her shoulder blade before she sat up, eyes flicking past me to where Thomas was also now sitting up, rubbing a hand over his face.

"Morning," she said, a little breathless.

Thomas silenced the alarm. "We should get ready. Sunrise is in twenty minutes."

I swung my legs out of bed and stood quickly, turning my back on both of them as I adjusted my shorts and willed my body to behave.

Cold air helped. Marginally.

"Bathroom," I said, already moving. "Calling it.

Shotgun. Whatever system we're using."

I glanced back once. Poppy's mouth tipped into a small, satisfied smirk, eyes bright with far too much understanding.

I didn't check if they were following to take their place by the door. I only hoped a quick cold shower would be enough to wipe the memory of that smile and those eyes from my mind.

* * *

The roof terrace was higher than I remembered.

We climbed the narrow staircase in silence, the stone cool beneath our boots, the air sharpening with every step. When the door opened, the cold hit us fully, crisp and biting, the kind that made your lungs ache on the first breath.

The terrace itself looked neglected. A scattering of potted plants, their soil dark and damp. Metal café chairs around a table with one uneven leg. Beyond the balustrade, the land stretched out, winter-bare and pale, the manor grounds rolling away into shadow. The sky was already lightening, bruised purple and blue.

I'd lived here for years, yet I couldn't remember the last time I'd stood up here and took in the beauty of the view.

Poppy stepped up beside me, pulling her coat tighter. She'd traded the thin tank top from the night before for an oversized hoodie and a thick green wool coat. I missed the view of her skin but had to admit that the color of the coat made her eyes startling, bright even in the low light.

Thomas moved with stiff purpose, crossing to the center of the terrace, "Here. That way is east."

We stood in a loose triangle, close enough that I could feel Poppy's warmth through her coat. She glanced at the sky, then at Thomas, nerves flickering across her face.

"Are you sure the words are... right?" she asked. "I mean, shouldn't they be in Old Norse or something? Latin? Or some ancient goddess language?"

Thomas shook his head. "The language doesn't matter. It's the intent that carries the magic."

She chewed her lip. "Okay. Just checking."

I reached out to take her hand, squeezing her gently to reassure her. "Don't worry. Lofn is very fluent in English."

Her head snapped toward me, one brow arching.

Thomas shot me a look, sharp and questioning, but the moment passed as he checked his phone again.

"Thirty seconds," he said.

The sky shifted almost imperceptibly. Birds began to stir, their calls tentative at first, then more confident. The horizon lightened, a thin blade of gold cutting through the dark.

"Now," Thomas said.

We spoke together.

"Under light's first truth," I said, my voice steady despite the strange pressure building in my chest, "I, Tristan Roswell, reject this bond and revoke this vow."

The words tasted wrong.

Sour. Heavy.

Hearing Poppy and Thomas say *reject*, hearing it aimed at me as much as anyone, sent a sharp twinge through my sternum that had nothing to do with magic. I felt Poppy's hand leave mine. The absence of it felt louder than the rejection itself.

The sun crested the horizon and light washed over us, pale and fragile. I felt it like a presence, the same hum in the air that accompanied Lofn's visits. Power, watching.

Then silence.

We stood there, breath fogging, waiting.

Poppy broke first. "Did it work?"

"Only one way to tell," I said.

Thomas nodded. "On my count we each take a step back." We'd been facing each other, close enough that our coats brushed. "One," Thomas said.

We stepped back.

Nothing.

"Two."

Another step. Still nothing.

"Three."

We took another step, then another, eyes locked, bodies tense. A faint, unfamiliar tickle in my chest, like static scratching at my insides.

We stopped at the edges of the terrace, the drop behind us close enough to feel dangerous. We'd taken about eight steps each, and while we'd been limited by the space on the terrace, I was starting to feel the clench in my chest that preluded the more intense pain.

"That's far enough," Thomas said, his own eyebrows pinching in discomfort.

Poppy let out a shaky laugh. "Well, trial one down, and it looks like we've maybe doubled our radius." Relief softened her face, her shoulders easing. Her excitement at the trial's success shouldn't have made me mad. I should have shared the feeling.

I didn't.

For Thomas's part, his expression had already turned pensive. I could almost hear the gears clicking into place. That look meant he was about to disappear into his books and theories and long hours of silence.

"Breakfast," I said quickly, hoping to avoid being dragged along with him. "We should eat."

Poppy's face lit instantly. "Yes. Please!" I offered her my hand without thinking, and she took it.

The three of us walked back down the stairs together, close again. And I smiled to myself, even as something deep in my chest ached.

CHAPTER 8

February 10
THOMAS

I told myself I was staying awake to work. It was the lie I'd been using for two nights now. The truth was simpler and far more irritating: even if I lay down, I wouldn't sleep. Not with her there. Not with the faint rise and fall of her breath threading the strawberry and jasmine scent of her through the dark.

The desk lamp cast a tight circle of light over my laptop and the scattered papers beside it. Outside the tall windows, the manor grounds were a frozen sweep of shadow and ice. February pressed in from all sides. Cold. Waiting.

I refreshed the forecast again.

Still nothing definitive. A low-pressure system forming offshore. Possibility it will move inland later in the week. I exhaled through my nose and closed the tab.

Two days since the dawn trial. Two days of learning the new edges of our radius. Two days of her presence threading itself into everything.

Behind me, the bed creaked softly.

I didn't turn. I already knew which sound was which now. Tristan slept like a stone once he went under, heavy and still. Poppy... didn't. She shifted. Mumbled. Kicked the covers off and dragged them back again. Like even sleep couldn't convince her to stay put.

I told myself not to look.

I failed.

She was on her side, facing the window, hair loose and tangled across the pillow. One arm was flung up above her head, the sleeve of her top riding high enough to show a strip of skin at her waist. I felt a pull to her that had nothing to do with the magic. Although that was there too.

I'd felt the magic loosen after the trial, like a knot easing. This was something else. A low ache in my gut that had been growing with every smart mouthed quip and impish grin.

I turned back to my work and forced myself to focus.

The advocacy brief on my screen had been stalled for weeks. A case involving two men imprisoned overseas under morality laws that hadn't been updated in decades. The legal argument was sound. The precedent solid. And still, something in it refused to cohere.

Earlier that afternoon, Poppy had wandered past my desk, mug of tea in hand, humming to herself.

"You look like you're trying to wrestle the words

into submission," she'd said.

"I am," I'd replied, without looking up.

She leaned over my shoulder anyway. Read for a moment. Then frowned.

"You're arguing it like the law is the be all and end all," she said. "But the politicians and lawyers don't actually care about the law. They care about perception and embarrassment."

I'd looked at her then.

She shrugged. "Make it expensive for them to keep pretending they're right. Socially, I mean. Shine a light they can't step out of without tripping."

It had been... annoyingly effective.

I'd rewritten half the framing since.

Now, staring at the revised draft, I felt the same reluctant admiration curl in my chest.

She wasn't trained in this. She didn't speak the language of institutions or policy. She just saw the pressure point and pressed.

A sound behind me cut through the thought. Not movement this time. A sharp, broken inhale. I was on my feet before I realized I'd moved.

Poppy was twisting in the sheets, her brow furrowed, breath coming too fast. One hand clawed at her throat, fingers digging into skin as if she were trying to pull something loose.

"Hey," I said quietly, sitting on the bed beside her and shaking her shoulder softly. "Poppy."

She didn't respond. I reached out before I could stop myself, brushing her hair back from her face. Her skin was warm under my palm.

"It's okay," I murmured, though I had no idea if it was true. "Wake-up."

Her eyes flew open.

For a split second, she looked at me like she didn't know where she was. Like she was bracing for something to close in. Then she sucked in a breath and focused.

"Oh," she said hoarsely. "It's you."

Something in my chest loosened at that.

"You were having a nightmare" I said.

She nodded once. Then looked around the room as if reassuring herself of her reality. "Yeah."

"You want to... um... talk about it?" I stumbled, my hand rubbing at the back of my neck. I had the irrational urge to hold her until she stopped trembling, but I didn't have the same easy report with her that Tristan did, and was worried my touch would not be welcome.

"Not really." She replied, the panic in her eye now receding quickly. She sat up, lifting her legs over the side of the bed and sitting beside me. She glanced toward the desk, the glow of the laptop catching her attention.

"You're still working?" she asked. "It's... late."

"I couldn't sleep. And was keeping an eye on the weather forecast for a storm." I replied. I was pretty sure that was the longest sentence I'd said to her since I'd met her.

"Any luck?"

"Possibly later in the week," I said. "Nothing guaranteed."

She smiled at that. Not wide. Just relieved. "I'll keep my fingers crossed then," she said. Then, quieter, "I don't think I'd survive another month of this."

The words were light. The truth underneath them wasn't.

"Can I ask you something?" She continued, her voice unsure. I was concerned her hesitancy was because my stand-offish behavior so far this week had left her worried I'd say no. So, I tried to relax my features into something a little more friendly as I encouraged her to go ahead and ask.

"After this is all over, the Order isn't going to disappear me, or anything, is it?"

I blinked. "What?"

"For knowing too much," she said. "You know, secret society, ancient goddess rituals."

A laugh escaped me before I could stop it. Low and surprised.

She leaned back shocked at my outburst, then rocked sideways, shoulder bumping into mine.

"Hey," she said, staring at me like I'd grown a second head. "Wow. Rude. It's a legitimate concern."

"You've been reading too many Dan Brown books," I said. "We're not that kind of organization."

She huffed. "You say that now."

"At most, you'll be asked to sign an NDA," I said. "Then you're free to go live your life."

She sobered at that. Just a flicker.

"Right," she said.

I saw the way she dipped her head, the way her fingers curled and picked at the blanket.

"What do you want to do when this is all over?"

"Before I got this *job*," she rolled her eyes at the word 'job', as the whole night guard thing had never really worked out. "I was kinda between gigs."

"Voluntarily?"

She snorted. "Not so much."

She told me, then. About her tennis career, and after it the position she'd taken at the club. Then the way she'd walked away from the polished fakeness of that without a plan and somehow trusted the world to catch her. I was filing away the details of her history like artifacts—carefully, deliberately, unwilling to lose any of them.

I found myself leaning closer without realizing it. Not because of the drama of it. But because she shared it all without self-pity. Without apology. As if choosing herself had been the most obvious thing in the world.

I had built my entire life on structure. On duty. On inherited systems.

The idea of choosing something simply because it felt right was... arresting.

"I don't really know what's next," she admitted, on a yawn. "But I admire how resolute you and Tristan are in your callings here."

"I began this work because it was what my parents did," I said. "They died doing it. But I do love it. Love knowing we're making a real differ—."

Before I could finish my sentence, I felt her head tip sideways and rest against my shoulder. Her breathing soft and even.

I froze.

Then, slowly, carefully, I shifted her back down onto the pillow. She murmured something unintelligible and began tossing again.

I hesitated, looked for a second at the expanse of space on the other side of the bed where I had rested the previous two nights. But instead of moving over there, I squeezed myself in to lay down beside her. She curled into me without waking, her forehead pressing into my chest, her hand fisting in my shirt. And her tossing and shuffling relaxed.

On her other side, Tristan slept on, oblivious.

I stared at the ceiling, heart pounding, and wondered when exactly this had stopped being a complication and started being something else entirely.

And why Lofn had decided I deserved it.

CHAPTER 9

February 11
TRISTAN

T he tennis court hadn't been used in years. Cracks webbed through the green surface, pale lines breaking it into uneven panels. The net sagged slightly in the middle, and the wind worried at it incessantly. The serving machine sat at the baseline, dented metal and peeling paint, humming with a tired persistence.

Poppy didn't seem to notice any of it.

She stood at the edge of the court, jacket already shed and tossed aside, breath puffing in white bursts as she bounced lightly on the balls of her feet. Leggings. Thermal top. Hair pulled back into a messy ponytail that had already started to loosen.

The machine spat the ball. She stepped into it and struck, clean and sharp. The sound cracking through the cold air again, and again, and again.

Thomas and I stood on the sideline of behind her. Heavy coats. Gloves. Scarves pulled high over our mouths. I stamped my feet, trying to keep the blood flowing.

"She's going to freeze," I muttered.

Thomas didn't take his eyes off her. "She knows what she's doing."

Another ball. Another strike. Her movements were a steady rhythm, precise and economical. No showboating. No wasted energy. Just motion and breath and focus.

"She needed this," Thomas said quietly. "You've seen her the last two days."

I had. The restless pacing. The way she hovered at the edge of rooms, fingers tapping against her thigh, jaw tight. Following us from meeting to library to planning session, pretending she didn't mind, pretending she wasn't climbing the walls.

"I know," I said. "I just don't love the idea of her getting hypothermia."

Thomas huffed a breath into his scarf.

I glanced at him. His nose was red. His shoulders were hunched against the cold. And still, his body angled toward her without conscious thought.

Another ball flew. Poppy pivoted and returned it, then the machine sent the next one too fast, forcing her into a scramble. Despite a valiant lurch for the ball, she missed it with a laugh. She caught her breath, hands on her knees, then straightened and looked at us.

"You two look miserable," she called.

"And you look like you are having a great time," I called back.

She grinned. "Will you survive just a few minutes more? I swear I'm almost done."

Thomas lifted one gloved hand in surrender. "Do what you need."

She went back to it, and for a while we just watched.

There was something grounding about seeing her like this. The way her body knew exactly what to do. The way the tension bled out of her with every swing. She wasn't performing. She wasn't trying to impress. She was simply... herself.

"She's remarkable," I said before I could stop myself.

Thomas shifted his weight, boots crunching faintly against the frozen grit at the edge of the court. All the while his eyes stayed on Poppy.

"Have you told her of your visions from Lofn? And the most recent where she forewarned this whole thing?" Thomas asked.

There it was.

We'd been standing out here for almost an hour as Poppy trained, and the whole time I had known there was something on his mind. But had also known better than to push him.

I looked back at the court, at the way Poppy moved through the cold like it was nothing, breath steady, body sure. "You know I haven't."

"I didn't know for sure. You... seem to... spend more time with her I guess," he fumbled, and I wondered if it was envy, he was struggling with, or guilt. Thomas often came across as a bit of a dismissive brute, but I'd learned over the years that the furrows in his brows were generally frustration with himself more than with others.

"Well, we're all spending time together," I laughed, gesturing between the three of us and the invisible spell that bound us.

"That's not the point," he replied. He exhaled, slow and controlled, like he was choosing his words with care. "Why haven't you told her?"

I got the impression he already knew the answer but wanted me to say it anyway.

"Because I don't want her to feel more trapped than we already are. These trials give her an out at the end. But the way Lofn described it, I don't think it is supposed to be temporary."

"But is that what Lofn actually said?" Thomas was quiet for a beat, then added, "This whole thing has been so strange. Why would Lofn's game take away our autonomy to choose?"

"She said we can't continue to preach about love when we have never felt it," I said, a little more tightly than I meant to.

"I'm not saying Poppy isn't important," Thomas went on. "Or that this—" he gestured toward the court, the rings on our hands, the ridiculousness of all of it, "—isn't meaningful."

His jaw tightened. "I'm just saying if she ever finds out we knew something that big and didn't tell her..."

He let the words hang and the silence between us stretched.

I swallowed. "I don't want to scare her."

"Or lose her?" Thomas asked, his tone softer now.

"I like her," I almost whispered it. "Outside of all of this."

Thomas continued to watch her. "I know," he said.

I studied him. The way his gaze tracked her without seeming to. The way his shoulders had eased at the same rate the tension in Poppy's had. It reminded me of the way Blair and Page had mirrored each other.

"You know, you're allowed to 'spend time with her' too," I offered.

He shot me a look. And while his glare demanded silence, I couldn't help but add: "Lofn did say that all this was for you too."

Poppy jogged over before he could reply. She was breathless and flushed as she tugged her jacket back on.

"Okay," she said, teeth chattering now that she'd stopped moving. "I concede. You win. I'm freezing." Relief washed through me.

"Inside," Thomas ordered.

She laughed. "Bossy."

"Concerned," I corrected.

She rolled her eyes but headed for the manor without argument. We followed, grateful for the shelter as the heavy doors shut behind us.

The gym was tucked into one of the newer wings of the building. It wasn't open to the public but had been recently renovated for the use of the Order members who shared the manor. It had polished concrete floors. Exposed beams. A row of tall windows that let in pale winter light.

Poppy peeled off her jacket as her eyes roamed the room. "You know, when you told me there was a gym, for some reason I had pictured some janky dumbbells and an old Stairmaster. You could have told me it was this... modern."

"We did." Thomas and I said in unison.

Poppy laughed at us, but I was concerned at the level of teeth chattering that her humor hid.

"There's a shower down here too," I said. "It's... larger than the ones upstairs."

She glanced past me, at the tiled doorway, then back again. The hesitation was brief, but real.

"Yeah," she said finally. "That would probably help."

* * *

Larger was an understatement. The shower room was an open expansive space that was larger than our kitchen. It had several showerheads set at different heights, protruding from dark tile walls, a natural stone on the floors.

We stopped just inside, and the reality of the space seemed to register on us all at the same time.

For the past two days, we'd enjoyed the extra space the first trial had gifted us. But our radius had only grown to about twelve feet. And with the layout of the bedroom and ensuite, it still meant we each showered with the other two still waiting outside the door, pretending not to listen.

Pretending not to be imagining what steam looked like on her skin. Pretending like I wasn't quickly becoming addicted to the scent of her soap, or that I wasn't taking a few extra minutes in the shower myself to jerk off with that very soap.

I'd grown up around every kind of love imaginable. The Order didn't flinch at orientation or configuration. Thomas and I had both lived enough life to know attraction didn't obey neat lines. I'd kissed men. I'd wanted men. I'd wanted women more often.

I had never wanted anyone the way I wanted her.

And now this shower — wide open, the doorway too far away for our radius— felt less like an inconvenience and more like a test.

She was cold. And every selfish part of me wanted to warm her.

Poppy glanced around, then back at us. Her breath still came a little fast from the cold and the workout, color high in her cheeks.

"Fuck it," she huffed, rubbing her hands together once. "I'm officially frozen. I can't wait until we get back upstairs."

She stepped past us before either of us could respond and reached for the controls, twisting the nearest dial. The pipes groaned briefly, then water thundered to life, hot almost immediately. Steam began to rise, slow and steady, blooming toward the ceiling.

She didn't step under it right away. For half a second, I considered turning around and giving her some semblance of privacy.

But she turned back to us, eyebrows lifting in a quiet, unmistakable invitation.

"You two coming," she asked lightly, "or just going to stand there and supervise?"

I met her gaze, and Thomas stepped closer beside me. She let her eyes travel between us, heat steady and deliberate. Then she nodded.

That was all the permission I needed.

I stepped forward first. Stripped off my coat, my jumper, set them aside. The air kissed cold against skin that had been wrapped up all day.

Behind me, fabric shifted. A zipper. The soft thud of boots hitting tile.

I didn't turn yet. I didn't trust myself to.

The water came on with a rush, steam blooming instantly. I stepped beneath it, heat striking my shoulders hard enough to draw a breath from my lungs. It soaked into muscle and bone, chased the cold away in long, indulgent waves.

When I opened my eyes again, she was there.

Her jacket was gone. Her hoodie too. She stood in a simple tank and leggings, hair already loosening from its tie, curls beginning to frizz in the damp air. She looked... real. Solid. Warm.

My body answered before my mind could intervene.

She moved closer, not touching yet. Just enough that I could feel her heat, the nearness of her, the way the bond tightened slightly as if pleased.

I became acutely aware of Thomas then. Of the way he filled the room without speaking. Thomas didn't look at me. He looked at her. His gaze tracked her with the same quiet intensity I felt in my own chest.

And there was no competition in it. No edge. Just the same hunger I felt.

I leaned in and kissed her hungrily.

She made a soft sound against my mouth and kissed me back, fingers curling into the fabric still clinging damply to my shirt. Heat flared, sharp and immediate, my body responding with a certainty that startled me.

And then Thomas was there. Not between us. Not taking over. One of his hands settled at her back, and his mouth brushed her shoulder, reverent and restrained, she inhaled sharply, her grip on me tightening.

She arched into us, and we closed around her without thinking. My hand tangled in her damp curls. Thomas's palm banded around her waist. We kissed her slow and thorough, like we were memorizing the taste.

I pulled back just enough to look at her. To be sure.

Her eyes were bright, pupils blown wide, lips flushed from the kiss. She looked down at Thomas's hand tightening at her waist, and then to her own hand resting on my chest, and the ring that gleamed under the streaming water.

"Wait," she whispered.

Thomas stilled instantly.

The water roared around us, heat pouring down my spine.

"Is this real?" she asked, voice barely audible over the spray. "Or is it just the bond?"

The question hit harder than any lightning.

For me? There was no hesitation.

It was real. It had been real from the rooftop. From the way she laughed. From the way she argued. From the way she looked at Thomas like she saw straight through him.

And I knew—without him ever saying it—that Thomas felt it too. I'd seen it in the way his jaw tightened when she smiled. In the way he watched her when he thought no one noticed.

But doubt changed things.

If she wasn't certain, if she thought this was just the magic—

Then we had no right to touch her. I met Thomas's gaze over her shoulder. He gave the smallest nod. Agreement. Restraint.

"You're right," I said, the words scraping on the way out. "This isn't the time."

Her throat worked.

Thomas's hand slid from her back. Mine followed a second later, fingers reluctant.

We stepped apart and stayed like that a minute longer, letting the heat do its work.

The space between us felt larger than it had any right to be.

CHAPTER 10

February 11
POPPY

I handed back Thomas's coat as I stepped out of our shared ensuite bathroom, grateful now to be warm in fresh clothes after the gym shower. My skin still felt sensitized, like it still remembered the way their hands had felt.

"I'm starving," I announced, too brightly, hoping to redirect the energy that still hummed between us.

Tristan's mouth twitched like he knew exactly what I was doing. "How about I rustle us up some sandwiches and we can settle in to watch a movie?"

We all agreed, maybe a little too quickly.

We fell into step down the hall in a new rhythm. Thomas walked beside me, close enough that our shoulders brushed when we turned corners. His hand flexed once at his side before he seemed to think better of reaching for mine. Tristan moved ahead of us, already debating bread options, but I caught the way he glanced back, checking—always checking.

I realized I was smiling anyway.

That was when Seraphine stepped into our path.

She looked immaculate, as always. Tailored jacket. Hair smooth. Lipstick untouched. But there was a tightness around her mouth that hadn't been there before, and her clipboard was clutched just a little too firmly against her chest.

"Good," she said, brisk. "There you are."

Tristan slowed instantly, attentive. Thomas straightened. I hovered half a step back, instinctively giving her space.

"We need to go over tomorrow evening," Seraphine continued. "The donors arrive at six. Cocktails in the east gallery. The Saint Valentine exhibit opens to them at seven sharp."

My phone buzzed in my hand.

I glanced down and felt a little jolt of relief. *Iris.*

"Sorry," I said, taking another step back. "I just need to take this—"

"This pertains to you as well," Seraphine said smoothly.

I stopped.

She looked at me then. Here eyes were measuring and calculating. But there was stress, flickering beneath the polish. The weight of a hundred moving parts balanced on her shoulders.

I declined Iris's call.

"Okay," I said, forcing brightness. "How can I help?"

Seraphine inclined her head, as if that were the

correct answer to a test, I hadn't known I was sitting.

"The museum is privately booked tomorrow night," she went on. "Cocktail dress. You'll be greeting guests alongside Tristan and Thomas."

I swallowed.

"Given the... circumstances," she added, with a slight tightening of her jaw, "your presence is unavoidable. And given your... adaptability these past few days, I'm prepared to acknowledge that you'll be an asset rather than a liability."

That might have been praise. From Seraphine, it was practically a bouquet.

Tristan shot me a quick, reassuring glance. Thomas nodded once, already slotting the information into place.

"We'll handle it," Tristan said. "Everything will be ready."

Seraphine exhaled, the barest crack in her armour. "Good. Because the success of this dinner matters."

She didn't need to say *to me*. The implication hung there anyway. When she finally left, I blew out a breath.

"I'm going to call my sister back," I said trying to shake off the feeling that some of Seraphine's stress had just leaked into my shoulders.

Thomas pulled out a stool at the breakfast bar without comment. I hopped up beside him, phone already to my ear, while Tristan moved into the kitchen and started pulling things from the fridge with the focused intensity of a man on a mission.

"Iris," I said. "Sorry. What's up?"

"You," Iris said, flustered. "You're what's up."

I could hear clattering in the background. Laughter. And Merry's unmistakable voice.

"It's Daisy's bachelorette tomorrow," Iris continued. "And Mom is being—well. Mom."

I closed my eyes briefly. Shit!

Daisy's bachelorette party was tomorrow. How did I forget that?

"Okay," I said calmly. "Deep breath. What's she done?"

"She's invited Mrs. Caldwell's daughter."

I groaned. "The neighbor?"

"We both know this is just the opening move. She's been trying to sneak in extra invites to the wedding for months. If we let this slide, Daisy might just succumb, and Mom will have the whole street seated right next to the cake."

I nodded in agreement. "Look, between you and me we can run interference. If we keep the neighbor girl away from Daisy, she won't get attached, then feel no guilt or pressure to invite her, or the rest of her family for that matter."

Merry's voice cut in, loud and cheerful. "Tell Poppy not to worry! I've got the penis confetti situation fully under control."

I smiled despite myself. Merry might be Daisy's best friend, but I'd always liked that girl.

"I'm so sorry I'm not there helping quality control the girth and colour of said penis confetti," I laughed. "I swear, if I wasn't—"

"Magically handcuffed to two very attractive men?" Merry supplied. "Tragic."

Thomas cleared his throat beside me. Tristan pretended very hard not to listen while slicing bread.

"You just get your butt to the party on time," Merry went on. "And maybe convince at least one of those men to join us for body shots. I'm flexible on which one."

"I'll see what I can do," I said dryly.

When I hung up, the kitchen felt quieter.

"I *can* do both," I said, before anyone could ask. "Right?"

"You mean body shots off both of us? Depends, do you mean at the same time, or one after the other?" Tristan responded with a surprisingly straight face.

"Well, that's something I definitely want to put a pin in to circle back to later. But I meant the dinner and the party. If the dinner wraps by nine, we can still book it across town and make it?" I wished it didn't come out as a question, that I had more certainty I wasn't going to mis my baby sister's bachelorette party.

"We can," Thomas reassured immediately. "These things rarely run late, especially on a Monday night."

I tried to let their certainty comforted me. Instead, my chest tightened.

I thought of my mother. Not as she was now, brittle and sharp-edged, and manipulative, but the version I'd seen once on an old home video. Laughing on a tennis court. Loud. Alive. The woman who had looked like she took up space without apology.

That woman hadn't survived her marriage to my father.

I watched Tristan and Thomas move around the kitchen, already planning, already sure.

I wanted to believe them.

I really did.

But something in me stayed alert. Waiting.

CHAPTER 11

February 12
THOMAS

After the gym, after the shower, after the way Poppy's mouth had opened under Tristan's and the way she had leaned into me and my touch too, I'd expected things to feel... different. Charged. Hungry. Restless.

Instead, yesterday evening had gone quiet.

We ate. We reviewed Seraphine's checklist for the dinner. Tristan tried to coax a smile out of Poppy with a story about a couple who'd insisted on exchanging vows beside a live falcon because the bird represented 'freedom'. Poppy had laughed in the right places. She'd said the right things. But then she'd drifted to the edge of the room like she was testing the limits of the new radius just to prove she could.

When we went to bed, she'd turned toward the window and stayed there.

Tristan had also fallen asleep fast, breathing deep, one hand lax over the blanket. I however, had lain awake for hours with my thoughts scraping the inside of my skull.

I told myself she was overwhelmed. I told myself she was tired. I told myself it was the rings, the lack of choice, the absurdity of being bound to two men she'd known less than a week.

Then my mind offered up a quieter possibility.

Did I do something wrong?

It didn't matter that I hadn't even been the one to kiss her first. It didn't matter that I'd held back when every animal instinct in me wanted to drag her closer. I still somehow felt responsible.

This afternoon, while Seraphine ran through the final seating plan, I'd caught Poppy staring into her coffee like it had personally betrayed her. When I asked if she was okay, she'd looked up too quickly and smiled too bright.

"Fine," she'd said. "Just thinking about... stuff."

Stuff was where she hid the truth.

And I'd let her, because asking risked an answer I wasn't ready to hear.

The museum had been transformed for the evening. Display cases glowed under softened lights. Velvet ropes guided guests like a slow current. Hired waitstaff moved with practiced calm. Glassware chimed. Laughter rose and fell like waves against stone.

Poppy wore a black dress that should have been simple, but on her it looked like a dare.

It barely reached her knees and clung to her hips in soft drapes of fabric. Her hair was half pinned back, the rest loose in soft curls that brushed her bare shoulders when she moved. She'd added small gold hoops and a delicate chain around her throat. Nothing flashy.

And still, she drew eyes. I watched a man with a silver beard turn his head when she passed. A woman in a deep green gown looked her up and down and smiled like she approved. Poppy returned the smile automatically, as if her body knew how to play this part.

Seraphine had underestimated her. Sure, she could be loud and a little wild, but she could also read people like she read her puzzles. She could charm them without trying to. Tonight though, it was like she was doing it all with the volume turned down.

Tristan stood at her other side, looking too pretty for his own good in a charcoal suit. His tie was a shade darker, hair pushed back from his forehead. His eyes kept flicking to Poppy too. The look of concern on his face telling me I wasn't the only one who noticed a shift in Poppy. The curse may keep our bodies close, but it did nothing to calm the way a person could drift from you emotionally.

I checked my phone for the hundredth time, waiting for my meteorology app to update. There'd been a growing likelihood of a storm only a few miles away, but with the obligations of the evening, I hadn't wanted to mention it to anyone until I was certain.

"Phone away," Seraphine scalded as she approached. I'd obeyed. Of course I'd obeyed. But it didn't stop my hand from brushing my pocket every few minutes like my phone was an itch I was told not to scratch.

Seraphine's expression was composed, but I could see the strain in small places: the set of her shoulders, the way her fingers flexed once before she clasped her hands.

She stopped in front of Poppy and looked her over, assessing.

Then, to my surprise, she nodded once. Approval.

"You're doing well," she said, voice low enough only we could hear. "All of you."

Poppy blinked. "Thank you."

Seraphine's gaze shifted to me. "Thomas. Bishop Noland is here, just on your left. I want you to meet him."

I'd read his work. Cited it. Argued with it in the margins of my own drafts. He wasn't just a donor or a guest. He was a gate. If I impressed him tonight, doors would open.

Seraphine's expression sharpened. "And please," she added, "try to look less like you're about to interrogate someone."

Tristan made a small sound that could have been a laugh, but he smothered it quickly with a cough.

Even Poppy's mouth twitched too.

"I'm always approachable," I said defensively.

Seraphine, Tristan, and Poppy, all gave me a similarly pointed *who are you kidding?* looks that I found mildly offensive. But I brushed it off and let Seraphine lead me to Bishop Nolan.

As we walked, I felt the faint tug in my chest that marked distance. The rings boundary flexible enough after the dawn trial that I could move around the room without pulling Tristan and Poppy right behind me like a leash. Still, the awareness of them never left me. A constant pressure behind my ribs.

Bishop Noland stood nearby looking at the Saint Valentine portrait. He was tall, immaculate, and smiling as he spoke to a cluster of historians. When Seraphine introduced me, he offered his hand.

"Thomas Lockhart," he said. "I've heard excellent things."

I returned the handshake. "I've read your work."

His smile widened. "A dangerous thing to admit."

Seraphine's laugh was soft, practiced.

The conversation that followed was exactly what it needed to be, and exactly what I hated.

Polished. Circular. Full of careful words and implied meaning. I spoke about the Order's legal advocacy, about our partnerships, about the practical need for protected rites in countries where same-sex partnerships could still be punished.

Bishop Noland asked questions that sounded curious but were designed to measure. I answered them, matching his cadence.

Seraphine watched, pleased.

At one point she leaned in and murmured, "Good. Keep going."

I did.

My mind kept pulling, though. Straining back

toward the edge of the room where Poppy stood beside Tristan, smiling at strangers.

I saw her laugh once, bright and quick. It was like a match struck in a dark space.

Then it faded. She looked down at her hand, thumb worrying the ring like she could rub it off if she tried hard enough.

I wanted to go to her. I wanted to ask what she was thinking. Instead, I stayed where Seraphine had placed me and performed.

Hours passed in fragments.

A toast. Applause. A discussion about relic provenance. A donor who wanted to tell me about his third wife's spiritual awakening in Bali. I smiled. I nodded. I spoke when spoken to.

And beneath it all, I kept checking my weather app for a storm.

It was irrational, in a way. Storms were weather. They didn't care about my schedule. They didn't care about Poppy's sister's bachelorette party. They didn't care that Valentine's Day was three days away and our final trial was timed to it.

Still, I'd been watching the forecasts like an addict. In my pocket, my phone might as well have been a pulse.

When the tightness in my chest sharpened, I looked around instinctively. Tristan was still in his chair near the center of the table, posture straight, smile polite. His hand had gone to his sternum, fingers pressing lightly. He met my eyes, and I saw the question there.

Where is she?

My gaze swept past him.

Poppy's seat was empty.

For a second, my mind went blank with a kind of animal alarm.

Then I spotted her.

She stood near the wall, half-hidden behind a tall floral arrangement, her phone lifted to her ear. She was speaking softly, shoulders angled away from the room, one hand curled at her throat like she was trying to hold down the pain of the stretched bindings.

I watched her face as she listened. The polite mask slipped. Something raw passed through her eyes. I couldn't hear her reply, but I could read the shape of them on her mouth.

Sorry. I'm trying.

A vibration buzzed against my thigh pulling my attention from her. It was an alert from the weather app. My fingers found my phone, my eyes darting around to make sure Seraphine wasn't watching. Even going as far to shield the screen with my palm like I was committing a crime.

The notification was what I was waiting for, the storm cell had finally developed.

But what was beneath it was not as welcome news—9:20 PM.

The numbers hit me like a blow to the chest that was wholly different from the feeling of the curse. Guilt and shame hollowed out my insides. No wonder Poppy was speaking so frantically into her phone. We were at least 20 minutes overdue to be leaving for her party.

I looked up to see her end the call and start walking back toward the table, her smile already returning. Practiced and falsely cheerful.

Tristan's gaze tracked her too, relief flashing across his face when the tug eased.

She saw me watching and adjusted her trajectory to come over to me. Tristan also got up from his chair to meet where I was standing.

Looking at my phone open in my hand Poppy asked, the first spark of genuine happiness brightening her face, "Are we ready to go?"

Tristan blinked and looked at his own watch, a curtain of guilt falling over his face too as he saw the time.

"Yes, we need to leave," I answered, hating that I was going to be the one to soon snatch that spark away.

Her smile held. "Okay. Cool. Iris's is about forty minutes from here. If we go now, we can still—"

"We aren't leaving for the party."

The words landed between us like dropped glass. Poppy blinked once. Twice. Then she nodded, slow. Her expression shattering.

Tristan just looked at me with an eyebrow raised.

"The storm," Poppy said, her voice flat.

I hated how quickly she understood. How quickly she gave in.

"Yes," I said. "We can't miss it."

Tristan stepped closer to her. "Couldn't we—"

He stopped when I cut my gaze to him. Just a fraction. A warning.

I looked back at Poppy.

"I'm sorry," I said. "I know this matters. I know we promised. But lightning storms in February aren't common. If we miss this, we could be waiting weeks. And we can't complete the new moon trial until we've completed this one first."

Her eyes flicked to Tristan, then back to me.

There was no argument in her face. No dramatic anger. Just something dimming. The light which had already been low all evening, all but extinguished now. I reached out without thinking, my hand moving to cup her jaw. My thumb aching to trace along her cheek bone. But she shifted away before my fingers could touch.

She took a step away from Tristan too. Her voice flat as she said, "Just let me get my coat."

And with that she walked off.

The curse tugged at my chest as she moved away. Not painful. Not yet. But it was a sudden reminder of distance.

Tristan stared after her, jaw tight.

"She's going to hate us," he muttered.

"I know," I said.

And worse, I knew I deserved it.

We left through a side corridor, slipping out before Seraphine could redirect us again. My mind registered her pleased glance from earlier, her trust, the promotion paths opening. All the platitudes and small talk I'd shared with Seraphine's guests felt pointless in my mouth now. Ashy.

Outside, the cold slapped us awake. Poppy was already at the car, coat on, hood up, arms crossed. She didn't look at us as we approached.

As we drove, the storm built around us. Rain hit the windshield like thrown gravel and country roads stretched ahead, black and slick. Poppy's phone kept lighting up in the back. And I could feel her frustration as she manically typed and erased and typed again.

Tristan twisted in his seat once, looking back at her. "Pop—"

"Please," she said, voice sharp. "Just… don't."

He went still.

I kept my hands tight on the wheel.

A streak of lightning split the sky, white-blue, illuminating the forest like a photograph. Thunder cracked a second later, close enough to make the car vibrate. The storm cell warning hadn't been exaggerating.

We turned into a dirt lot marked by a small wooden sign for a trail. Trees crowded in on all sides. The rain was heavier here, sheets of it. Wind whipped branches overhead.

I killed the engine and for a moment, none of us moved.

"This is it," I said.

Poppy opened the door immediately.

Rain slammed into her, but she didn't break stride as she stepped out and started walking into the woods, boots crunching on wet gravel, hood pulled low.

"Poppy," Tristan called.

She didn't turn.

The tightness in my chest sharpened. Not pain yet. The warning. Tristan and I scrambled out, the cold biting hard now that the car's warmth was gone. Rain soaked through my coat within seconds. Poppy kept going, fast, like she was trying to outrun something.

The curse didn't allow it.

The moment she crossed the edge of our radius, pain flared hot and bright, straight through my sternum. I gritted my teeth and forced my legs forward, chasing the inevitable. Because the storm was here. The trial was here.

And whether it broke us or freed us, there was no stepping around it now.

CHAPTER 12

February 12
POPPY

Rain sheeted through the trees, cold and sharp, soaking my hood within seconds. Wind tore at my coat, shoving at my shoulders, pushing leaves and needles against my legs as if the forest itself wanted to drive me back. Lightning flared somewhere to my left, bleaching the trunks white for a heartbeat before plunging everything back into shadow.

Good.

Let it rage.

The clearing opened suddenly, a ragged circle of earth and leaf litter churned dark by the rain, ringed by trees that bent and groaned overhead. At the far edge of the clearing, half-swallowed by shadow, sat a pair of weathered wooden picnic tables. They appeared like old, solid things, slick with rain and scarred by years of use.

The air seemed to buzz, and my all my nerves felt too close to the surface, oversensitive and firing at every raindrop that hit my skin.

"This is it," Thomas said, coming up behind me, his voice raised over the wind.

I turned to look at him. Rain soaked his coat, darkening the wool, and beading in his beard along the sharp line of his jaw. His hair was plastered back from his face, eyes bright in the lightning-dark. He looked less like a scholar and more like something dragged straight out of a viking saga.

Tristan came up on my other side, breathless from chasing me from the car. His hair curling as the rain soaked him, leaving water tracking down the line of his throat and disappearing beneath the collar of his shirt.

The worst part was how my body responded to the sight of the two of them, even as my mind rebelled. Even as the anger sat in my chest, even as I craved space, distance, and freedom enough to breathe. There was something sharper, more dangerous under it all, pulling at me to step closer, instead of away.

The storm pressed in, heavy and waiting. Lightning flickered through the trees, close enough that the air felt alive with it. Thomas was right. This was it. Whatever I was feeling—desire, fury, fear—it didn't matter anymore. I nodded once and we moved into position, boots sinking into mud. Lightning cracked again, closer this time. Thunder followed almost immediately; a deep, chest-rattling boom that made my teeth click together.

"You remember the words?" Thomas shouted.

I nodded, not trusting my voice. Beside me I saw Tristan nod too, his arms wrapped tightly around his body to try and keep the wind out of his coat.

"Together, then," Thomas instructed.

The rain plastered my hair to my cheeks, slid down my neck, soaked straight through my clothes. My hands were numb with cold, fingers stiff and clumsy as I fisted them in the pockets of my coat. I could feel Tristan beside me without looking. Solid. Steady. And I repressed the urge to lean into his warmth.

"Now," Thomas said.

We spoke together.

"Under love amid chaos," I said, voice shaking despite myself, "I, Poppy Everly, reject this bond and revoke this vow."

The word *reject* tasted wrong. Bitter. Like forcing myself to swallow something sharp.

Lightning answered us, a jagged white vein tearing the sky open. Heat surged through my chest, brighter than the lightning, sharper than the cold. The magic cracked outward, invisible but violent, like pressure finally being released.

Pain followed. Not the blinding agony from before. This was different. Deeper. A hot ache that bloomed under my ribs and radiated outward, setting every nerve alight.

I gasped. The air felt too thin. Too heavy. Like the storm had crawled inside my lungs. For a moment, I thought I might scream.

Then it eased.

And the easing was worse.

The hum in my chest loosened, stretched, as if someone had pulled my ribcage farther apart and left the cavity hollow. Cold rushed in where something warm had been. I swayed, suddenly unmoored, my body reaching for what it needed to sooth and comfort the sensations it was feeling.

Them.

The instinct hit hard and fast: step closer, close the gap, let them anchor me. Let them touch me and make the shaking stop.

The want terrified me.

My hands curled into fists. No. I was not going to run to them just because the magic had taught my body how good it felt to belong there.

"Did it—" Tristan started.

I didn't wait to hear the rest. I just turned and ran.

Branches whipped at my arms. Wet leaves slid under my boots as I tore through the trees, breath ripping out of me in harsh bursts. My legs knew what to do. Years of training took over, muscle memory burning clean and sure through the chaos in my head.

Run. Just run.

Behind me, someone shouted my name, but I didn't slow.

Rain blurred my vision. My chest burned. My lungs screamed. But the pain in my heart—the aching —drove me harder than the physical strain ever could.

The party. Daisy. Iris. My promise. Neither Tristan nor Thomas had remembered. Not until it was too late. I focused on these things, my brain wrestling with my heart to reinforce and remind myself of the facts as I pushed to run even faster.

The pressure in my chest flared suddenly, a tight, clawing ache that made me stumble. I caught myself on a tree, palms slapping wet bark as I bent forward, gasping.

Looks like I'd found the edge of the new radius.

I pressed my forehead against the trunk and sucked in air, rain dripping from my lashes. My heart hammered in my throat.

Footsteps crashed toward me. I turned to see Thomas burst through the trees first, rain streaming off his coat, breath rough, eyes blazing. He skidded to a stop inches from me and slammed his hand against the tree above my head, the impact jolting through the wood.

"What the hell were you thinking?" Thomas snarled.

I lifted my chin, breath still tearing in and out of me. "What do you care?"

The words were flat. Almost casual. Like I hadn't just run half a mile into the dark.

His eyebrows shot up for the briefest second, before crashing down again angrily over his storm-gray eyes. He had stopped so close I could feel the heat rolling off him, his chest heaving from the run. He filled the space in front of me solid and unyielding.

"What do I—" He cut himself off, a sharp, incredulous sound tearing out of his chest.

He loomed over me stepping even closer now,

broad and furious and terrifying in a way that made something reckless spark low in my belly. I tried to push him away, to find some space for my brain to cling to the anger that was quickly slipping away under his proximity. But despite putting considerable effort into my arms as I shoved at his chest, he remained immovable.

Tristan reached us a heartbeat later, breath ragged, eyes feral and bright. He came in close on my other side, not touching, but hemming me in, like if he left even an inch between us, I might bolt again. His hand hovered near my arm, then dropped, then lifted again, unsure.

I jerked my eyes from him back to Thomas, desperate for the anger now, for anything that wasn't the way my body was lighting up under their proximity.

"I'll tell you what I was thinking," I snapped. "I was thinking you'd both forget me. Again."

"That's not fair," Tristan said, fast and shaken.

"Isn't it?" I shot back. "Because from where I was sitting at that party, it felt a lot like I was expected to just... fall in line. Smile. Be understanding. And just accept that your work, and your ambitions were more important than mine."

Thomas's jaw clenched. "We didn't forget."

"You did," I hissed. "You both did. And the worst part?" My voice broke, fury cracking into something raw and exposed. "I almost didn't care. I almost convinced myself it made sense. I could feel myself shrinking. Justifying it. And I hate that. I hate how easy it was."

Lightning flashed, further away now, though the rain continued fall, making my words splutter as I scolded them. Tristan stared at me like I'd struck him.

"Damn it, Poppy" Thomas growled, his rough voice sending vibrations down my body and feeding the growing heat in my belly. "Do you think this is easy for us?"

I scoffed. "It looks pretty damn convenient."

His hand slammed into the tree again, closer this time, his body caging me in without actually touching. I watched as he clenched his eyes closed, taking a deep breath, and trying to calm himself before he spoke again. His next words were calmer, but no less rough and raw: "I have thought about you every minute since you walked into our lives. Every minute." He opened his eyes then, locking his penetrating gaze on me. "I've fought it. Rationalized it. Told myself it was the rings, the proximity." His voice cracked, just slightly. He lifted the hand that was not pressed into the tree to trace my cheek, pushing at a strand of my rain-slicked hair. "But it's not."

Tristan's hand too, no longer fretted in the space between us but landed on my shoulder and dragged down my arm.

Thomas's gaze burned into mine. "You don't get to accuse us of forgetting you when the truth is we're trying not to tear ourselves apart wanting you." His finger reached my jaw and moved to hold my chin between his thumb and finger, pulling my face to meet his eyes. "And you don't get to run from us. Ever."

My breath stuttered.

He released my chin, and his large hands engulfed my cheek as he cupped my face. Then my eyes went wide as he pulled me to him. He kissed me long and deep, our cheeks only inches from Tristan's face. The instant Thomas pulled back, Tristan used his grip on my arm to jerk me to him. Burying his hand in my wet hair,

"What he said," he said with a smirk before he leaned in to nip at my lower lip, demanding I let him in. When I took a breath, he pressed his tongue into my mouth and groaned. His body pressing closer like it was almost sagging with relief. He wrapped his arms around my waist, pulling me even tighter to him. And as much as I hated to admit it, the strength of his hold was like throwing gasoline on smoldering embers. I'd felt an instant physical attraction to Tristan, long before the rings had been involved. Now... in his arms... with Thomas's heavy hand stroking up my back, that initial spark was turning into an ache, a burning desire for more.

"What do you both think you are doing?" I huffed when Tristan finally released me, wishing my words sounded more insulted. Instead, my voice had gone husky and even I couldn't mistake the flirty dare I'd just issued. Tristan studied my face, looking far too pleased.

Damn, I was clearly failing to hide my lust.

Tristan didn't answer at first, instead he spun me around to face Thomas. Tristan's arms slid around my waist, pulling me back against his chest. His warmth worked through my soaked clothes, solid and anchoring. His breath brushed my ear.

"Perhaps it's time we stop acting like we want space, when really there's nowhere else we'd rather be than *inside* of you," he whispered into my ear, his voice vibrating along my skin.

My knees nearly buckled. And even if I wasn't certain that Tristan could hold me upright, Thomas stepped up, pressing his body to mine, adding his strength. We remained there, still as statues for what felt like eternity. Three people bound together, who only minutes ago swearing to the sky that we were rejecting each other, and I was struck by the bizarreness of our situation. If I wasn't so painfully aroused, desperate for their touch, I'd laugh at the absurdity.

Finally, Tristan's hands slid from my waist along to my hips, pulling my ass against his crotch, and I licked my lips as I felt the hard ridge of his cock.

Thomas's hands began to roam too, finding my breasts and cupping them. His touch burned through my wet clothing. Sandwiched between them, I realized how small I was compared to them. But I felt no fear, right then all I could think about was their touch and the throbbing sensation between my legs that ached for a release.

Thomas searched my face like he was memorizing my every reaction to his touch, then he kissed me. His mouth crashed into mine, rain-cold and hot-heat all at once, stealing my breath completely. I made a sound I didn't recognize, something broken and needy, and kissed him back just as hard.

From behind me, Tristan tightened his hold, his lips finding my neck, my jaw. His mouth was warm and reverent and hungry all at once, his hands pulling my hips tighter to his groin.

Prickles of heat zinged between my neck and breasts, making my nipples even more responsive to Thomas's rolling and pinching.

When Tristan's hands slid around and into my coat, drifting down my belly and lower to press through my dress and against my pussy, alarm bells signaled confusion in my brain. There were too many hands, too many sensations. I arched back into Tristan's hand without thinking, earning me a closer press into Thomas and the ridge of his cock into my stomach. Tristan's breath turned rough against my skin as his hands pressed harder, possessive now, claiming. Thomas made a low rough sound against my mouth, and then his grip shifted, decisive.

I sucked in a sharp breath as he pulled me from Tristan's grip and hauled me up and over his shoulder, my stomach jolting against his back.

"Hey—" I protested, breathless, my ass now up and on show. I could feel my coat ride up immediately, my dress with it, cool air brushing bare skin. "Put me down!"

He didn't. Instead, his hand tightened around my legs, thumb tracing small, deliberate circles on the soft skin of my inner thigh.

"This way you can't run again," he said, low and

clipped, already moving.

I let out an exasperated huff, then pushed up, pressing my palms into his back enough to see that Tristan followed close behind us, unhurried, eyes dark and intent. When our gazes caught, his mouth curved up into a smile that held no mirth, only hunger and the arrogance of one who knows exactly where his next meal was coming from.

The ground blurred beneath us, wet leaves, churned mud, roots slick underfoot. The rain had eased, thinning to a light patter that seemed insignificant to our already soaked-through clothes. Thunder rolled farther off, no longer overhead.

Thomas slowed only when we reached the edge of the clearing again. I was surprised when he didn't take us towards the car, but instead he carried me to the edge of the clearing and the picnic tables. The closest table loomed out of the wet dark, its surface slick with rain and scattered leaves.

Before he could lower me, Tristan stepped past us. Pushing up again to peer over Thomas's shoulder, I watched as Tristan shrugged out of his coat, then his suit jacket, and spread them across the tabletop. His white shirt clung to him now, soaked through. The inked shapes of his tattoos just visible where the translucent fabric clung across his shoulders and chest.

My breath hitched, even as my mouth watered.

Thomas's hand flexed on my thigh as if he felt it too, his thumb dragging once, slow and maddening, over bare skin before he finally lowered me onto the coats. The fabric was still soggy, but it was soft and warm, compared to how I imagined the wood beneath would be. And best of all it smelled like Tristan.

My pulse raced as I lie sprawled there under both their gazes.

The length of the picnic table pressed into my back, my legs hanging loosely at the knee over the edge. My dress had ridden up to almost my hips, and despite the rain-chilled my exposed skin felt hot.

Tristan settled at my right, perching on the bench that ran along the table's length. His hands brushing up my sides drawing up my arm up over my head, until I was gripping the far edge of the table. My other arm followed the first, his eyes slow and appreciative, as they took in the view of my sprawled form.

"Hmmm," he groaned, voice low and amused. "What a delicious feast you look, all laid out for us."

Heat flared in my belly.

Thomas stood at my feet. I watched as he shrugged out of his coat first, then his suit jacket, folding neither, just draping them over the opposite bench from Tristan's. His shirt was also soaked through. I could see the broad planes of his chest beneath it, the ridges and valley of defined muscle clear where the fabric clung to his broad shoulders.

Tristan was all ink and sharp lines, his muscles enhanced by the twisting lines he decorated his body with.

Thomas needed no enhancement. He was raw power—thicker through the chest, arms corded and heavy with strength, heat rolling off him even in the cold.

He stepped closer. His hands found my knees and drew them apart with calm inevitability, moving into the space between them.

"If she's our feast, then I think you should take a taste of her Tristan. Tell me exactly how delicious she is."

My breath stuttered, as obediently, Tristan unbuttoned my coast and lay it open, like I was a present he got to unwrap. He then tugged at the strapless front of my dress, pulling down my bra with it. The crisp air made my nipples pebble immediately, but they were quickly warmed as Tristan held the mound of one breast firm with one hand and took the nipple of the other into his mouth.

"She tastes unbelievable," he whispered against my breast, letting his tongue flick against my nipple with his words, before taking it back in his mouth and sucking harder, as if to prove his point. I felt a moan slip past my lips and my head fell back at the sensation.

Thomas pushed my legs wider, pushing my dress up to my waist and exposing my black lace thong to his hungry eyes. I was so wet, so ready, I was sure a single touch to my clit would send me over. As if he knew that, Thomas's hand stayed away, instead running his finger along the edges of the lace, the very tips of his fingers a teasing breath from the lips of my sex.

"Are these panties wet from the rain, or is this

all for us, Poppy?"

"Oh god," I gasped, Tristan's teeth having clenched down onto my nipple at Thomas' words and sending fire directly to my pussy.

"Answer me, Poppy." Thomas commanded.

"Yes, yes, it's for you."

"Good girl." Thomas soothed, bending until his lips touched my belly. His beard tickled my skin as he kissed his way down toward my pussy. Tristan looked up to watch the other man's descent.

The first touch of Thomas's tongue had me crying out, and Tristan's fingers squeezed tighter on my nipples at the same time, heightening the heat and pressure and pleasure of it all. Thomas's tongue was hot as he licked at my clit, his hands kneading at my hips, pulling me harder into his mouth with every stroke, flick, and press. My moans grew louder as I clutched at the table above my head. But just when I felt I was on the very crest of coming on his tongue, he pulled back. His breath still a warm caress across the flesh that desperately wanted more of his mouth. A wave of disappointment and shadow of my earlier rage coursed through me. But when I opened my mouth to berate him, to demand he satisfy me, Thomas spoke first.

"You are indeed a delectable meal, Poppy. You should taste for yourself."

And with his words, he rose and came up on my other side. Then he leaned down and kissed me, hard. His tongue brushed mine, and I could taste the salty sour taste of my arousal on it. While he continued to kiss me, he slid two fingers over my clit and along my slit, gathering more wetness and teasing me back closer to my climax. But, once again he pulled way before I could come, removing his fingers, and breaking our kiss. I followed the movement of his hand as he brought his slickened fingers to Tristan's mouth. I gaped in rapt wonder as I watched Tristan take Thomas's fingers, his eyes closing and his cheeks hollowing as he sucked them deeply, clearly wanting to savor every drop of the offering. A fresh flush of desire soaked at my thighs.

When Tristan opened his eyes again, they locked with mine and the heat in them caused my heart to beat harder.

"I think Poppy is looking a little hungry herself, Tristan." Thomas said, leaning back.

Tristan didn't respond, but the devious smile on his face seemed to say enough. He stood from the bench, somewhere along the line he had already unzipped his pants, but his boxers were still pulled up, and I could see the bulge of his cock under the fabric.

I felt one of Thomas's hands stroke my thigh, running his thumb up the inside sensitive skin. I looked down to see his other hand unzipping his pants now, too. When he slipped two fingers into my pussy, I shuddered and dropped my head back on the table.

Tristan brought my attention back to him, his hard fingers catching my chin, forcing me face to him.

"Come here gorgeous."

He'd already worked his boxers over his cock,

and it was rigid in front of my face, the head already wet with pre-cum.

I licked my lips, wondering what it would feel like to have his thick cock stretching my pussy. His fingers were gentle as he caressed my cheeks, his thumb brushing over my lower lip, before pressing into it and encouraging me to open my mouth, guided it to his cock. I didn't really need a lot of prodding though. I opened my mouth, swirling my tongue over the tip, then closing my lips around it.

I felt fingers run along my slit, spreading my wetness, and teasing my clit, before Thomas positioned his cock at my entrance. Tristan's fingers tightened in my hair as I moaned around his length.

It was dizzying trying to keep up with the movements of both men, trying to process the sensations they were both eliciting in my body.

Together they moved, Thomas's cock thrust into me with one hard push, while

Tristan's filled my mouth. I tensed against the onslaught of invasions, but in the next heartbeat, a wave of pleasure crashed over me. I closed my eyes and gave myself to them, to this amazing moment.

Thomas thrust in and out of my pussy in a steady, slow rhythm. Each plunge pushed me forward driving Tristan's cock deeper into my mouth, the head brushing the back of my throat.

My hands were white-knuckle tight as they gripped the edge of the table. Tristan's hand (the one not buried in my hair pushing him even deeper into my mouth), reached out and found my nipple. He pinched it, the rough touch sending lightning sparks straight to my clit and when Thomas stroked it, I came.

The orgasm ripped through me, tightening the muscles of my belly and pussy. I swallowed Tristan's cock, needing that fullness in both my mouth and my pussy as I rode the waves of pleasure.

I shuddered anew as Thomas drew his cock completely out of me, then thrust back in. His motions weren't slow and deep anymore, but now punishingly hard and fast, my whole body shaking from the force. A few thrusts later, I felt Thomas tense with his climax, his body falling over mine, and his breath coming out in ragged pants over my belly button.

"My turn," Tristan said.

I barely had time to understand what that meant when his cock was pulled from my mouth, and he was standing beside Thomas. I felt Thomas withdraw and move to the side and in the next breath, Tristan had gripped my hips, lifting them up as his cock thrust into me. I wrapped me legs around Tristan's waist on instinct. He didn't move at first, having to go slow to allow my orgasm-tight body to accommodate him.

Thomas took his place at my left side, his hand sliding along my belly until his fingers found my clit, rubbing it gently for several moments before moving lower. He touched the stretched flesh at my entrance where Tristan's cock slid into me, and I gasped for air. They had completely undone me with so many sensations, and I was struck by the realization there was nothing I would refuse these men if they asked.

Thomas's fingers continued to tease my entrance and then my clit in alternating cycles, until I returned to the height of another orgasm.

"Fuck," Tristan growled, head thrown back, eyes on the still cloudy sky. He was seated to the hilt, filling me with his hard flesh. "You're so fucking tight, Poppy."

"Can you come again, for us darling?" Thomas crooned in my ear.

"Yes, yes." My entire vocabulary had shrunk to that one word. It was all I needed. "Yes."

Tristan pressed in once more as Thomas applied even more pressure to my clit. Then it was over.

Or had it just begun?

This orgasm wasn't a surge of pleasure like the first. It was too intense to be given such a kind name. It ripped through me. I screamed out and my back arched as something so acute it was almost pain shattered me. Tristan continued thrusting into me, hard and fast as I heard him cry out his climax. Thomas now also sucking on my nipple with a pressure that hovered on the razor's edge between rapture and discomfort.

"No more, no more," I begged, my head thrashing from side to side. Tristan pulled out and dropped immediately to his knees, replacing his cock with his mouth. I gasped at the dirty act, knowing he'd be tasting the aftermath of all three of our orgasms.

Thomas's fingers and Tristan's tongue danced over my quivering clit, and I screamed again.

I wasn't sure if it was the same unending orgasm or if they had pushed me to a third climax, but I shook hard, my body succumbing to the glorious agony.

I reached out, needing something other than a table to ground me. My hands grasped at Tristan's head and Thomas's shoulder, and I clung to them as I splintered into a million tiny pieces.

When I had nothing more to give, my body went limp.

I was empty, exhausted, and completely overwhelmed.

I'm not sure who it was that picked me up and carried me to the car. I was just vaguely aware of a warm arms caging me to an even warmer chest. Then, wrapped in their arms, I fell into a deep, dreamless sleep as we drove home.

CHAPTER 13

February 13
TRISTAN

I woke with my arm numb and my heart too full. Poppy was half on top of me, one bare thigh slung across my hips, her hair a warm spill across my chest. Thomas lay on her other side, close enough that I could feel the steady heat of him through the blankets. Somewhere in the night we'd tangled ourselves together: first with very heated intention, then once we'd fallen asleep, we'd continued to tangle unconsciously too.

For a few seconds I didn't move. I just breathed.

The storm still lived in my bones. Rain, lightning, her fury. The way she'd looked at us like she might shatter or devour us whole. The way she'd kissed us like we could hold her together.

Poppy shifted, her nose brushing my collarbone.

"Morning," she murmured, voice rough and sleepy.

"Is it?" I asked.

She snorted softly. "Feels like tomorrow."

Thomas made a sound that might have been agreement. Or disapproval. Or both.

I smiled before I could stop myself.

Poppy tipped her chin up, green eyes blinking open. She took one look at my face and groaned. "Don't do that."

"Do what?"

"That thing where you look like this was all a very good idea."

I laughed. "It wasn't?"

She studied me for a beat, then softened. Her hand came up, fingers resting lightly over my heart. "It wasn't my best idea to run," she said quietly. "I'm sorry."

"You were hurting," I said.

"I still shouldn't have run."

Thomas shifted, propping himself up on one elbow. His hair was a mess, his expression unusually open. "You scared the hell out of us," he said. Then, after a pause, "But I understand why."

She met his gaze, something fragile flickering there.

"We're sorry about Daisy's party," I said quickly. "We should have remembered. We should have—" I stopped myself before the words tangled into excuses. "We failed you."

Poppy exhaled, long and slow. "Thank you for saying that."

For a moment the room went quiet again. Not awkward. Just... settled. Changed.

I became aware of the space between us. What little there was, still hummed with magic, but lower now, less insistent. We could have rolled apart if we wanted to. Even stand in separate rooms around the manor.

The thought left me cold.

Thomas seemed to feel it too. His eyes flicked briefly to the door, then back to Poppy. "We don't have to decide anything today," he said. "About... us."

Poppy's mouth twitched. "Good."

She slid out of bed a moment later, stretching like a cat, utterly unbothered by her nakedness or our attention. I watched her go with a dull ache under my ribs, equal parts contentment and fear.

When she disappeared into the bathroom, Thomas let out a breath. "You okay?"

I nodded. Then shook my head. "No."

He huffed a quiet laugh. "Same." We didn't say more. We didn't need to.

* * *

Seraphine found us in the library an hour later. Poppy was in the sitting room, phone to her ear, voice low. With the expanded radius, she could be there without pain now. But still the door between us was only partly closed.

Seraphine ushered in with brisk efficiency and closed the door behind her.

"I have good news," she said.

Thomas straightened instinctively.

"The dignitaries were impressed," she continued. "Deeply. They've extended a formal invitation. For joint research and ritual demonstrations across several sites." She smiled at Thomas. "Including Norway."

My pulse jumped.

"Both of us?" I asked.

She glanced between us, surprised by the question. "Of course, both of you. This is precisely the sort of work you've been preparing for."

"When?" Thomas asked.

"As soon as the Valentine exhibit closes.

The relics returned to their original homes from March. Just a few weeks away.

"And the ritual?" Thomas asked carefully.

She waved a hand. "Completed this weekend, naturally. There's no reason to delay. Things will return to what they were, and Poppy's time with us, while enlightening on many counts, will end. It's for the best."

I thought of Poppy in the next room. Of her laughter this morning. Of the way she'd looked at us in the rain, wild and breaking and alive.

"Yes, the best" I said, because I didn't know how not to.

Seraphine clasped her hands together, satisfied. "I'll make the arrangements."

When she left, the room felt too quiet.

Thomas rubbed his face. "This is what we wanted right?"

"It was." For the first time since Lofn had ever spoken to me, I wondered what it would cost to keep her.

"And now?"

I leaned back against the desk. For a moment, I couldn't find words that didn't feel selfish and petulant.

And now, a reckless part of me thought, *we could stall.*

Delay the third ritual. A technicality. A scheduling conflict. The Order would have to bend and bring Poppy with us. Make space for her.

For one reckless moment, I let myself imagine it anyway.

Planes and train schedules rearranged as easily as chess pieces. Poppy folded into our world the way I'd been folded into it years ago.

I could see her beside us at conferences, leaning close to whisper jokes under her breath. Wandering foreign streets with her hands in her pockets, eyes bright with curiosity. Nights with the three of us tangled and laughing, something fierce and real growing between us.

But the more I tried to build this shiny, happy picture, the more it slipped.

Her smile in my mind went tight at the edges. Polite. Practiced. The way it had been at the event last night, when she'd done everything asked of her and nothing more. I saw her standing just behind us, always half a step back, learning when to be quiet. When to soften. When to disappear.

I exhaled, the fantasy dissolving. I knew better. Whatever else this bond had become, it couldn't start with us deciding her life for her.

I rubbed a hand over the back of my neck. "And now we finish the ritual."

Thomas didn't answer right away. He moved to the window instead, hands clasped behind his back, staring out at the gray stretch of grounds beyond the glass.

"She won't come with us," he said.

It wasn't a question. "You don't know that."

He turned then, expression sharp but not unkind. "I do."

I pushed off the desk, restless. "We could make it work. We'd have time before the travel. We could talk to her. Explain—"

"Explain what?" he cut in. "That we want her to uproot her life to follow us from site to site? That the Order comes first? That it always will?"

"That's not fair," I snapped.

"No," he agreed. "It isn't. Which is the point."

Silence pressed in around us.

I dragged a hand through my hair. "I love her."

The words surprised me with their ease. With how true they felt once spoken.

Thomas's jaw tightened. He looked away again, just for a second. When he spoke, his voice was low.

"So do I."

Something in my chest cracked open and I stepped closer to him. "We don't have to choose between her and the work."

"Yes," he said immediately. Then, more gently, "We do."

I shook my head. "You're assuming she wouldn't want—"

"I'm assuming she knows herself," Thomas said. "And that she's been shrinking since the moment this began."

I stepped back again, leaning back on to the desk, as if his words had pushed me.

I thought of her at the dinner. The way her smile hadn't quite reached her eyes. The way she'd gone still when the storm alert came through.

"You felt it too," Thomas went on. "Last night. This morning. She's already bracing for the end."

I swallowed. "So, what? We just... let her go?"

He turned fully toward me now. "We finish the ritual. We give her back her choice. And if she stays —" His voice roughened. "Then she stays because she wants us. Not because magic cornered her into it."

I closed my eyes.

Lofn's voice echoed in my memory. *Love isn't a relic in a display case. It's a living thing.*

"It feels selfish," I said, hating how much it hurt. "To want to keep her with us anyway."

Thomas stepped closer, saying nothing but resting a hand on my shoulder. "But you're right. Tomorrow, we need to finish it."

CHAPTER 14

February 14
POPPY

Seraphine knocked just as I was wrestling with the clasp of the bracelet. It was delicate. Gold filigree. Too nice for me, really. But it had been a gift from my sisters last Christmas. I had it looped around my wrist, fingers fumbling, tongue caught between my teeth as I tried to angle the tiny hook into place without dropping the whole thing on the floor.

"Poppy?" Seraphine said, opening the door and sticking her head into the room.

"Yeah," I turned toward the door and dropped the damn bracelet.

She took in the scene in one glance: the dress laid out on the bed, my shoes kicked off under the chair, my hair half-pinned and already slipping free. Her gaze paused on the floor where the bracelet had fallen.

"May I?" she asked.

I picked it up and placed it in her outstretched

hand, then I held my arm out.

Her fingers were cool and precise, movements efficient in the way of someone who had fastened a thousand impossible clasps in her life. For a moment, we stood close enough that I could smell her perfume —something subtle and expensive, cut with vanilla.

The boys' voices drifted faintly from down the hall. Tristan's, light and easy. Thomas's lower murmur answering him.

Seraphine's mouth tightened, just a fraction.

"They're excited," she said.

"So am I."

She finished the clasp and didn't let go of my wrist right away. Instead, she turned it gently, as if checking her work.

"You've handled this week... better than I expected," she said.

That surprised me enough that I laughed. "Low expectations?"

A corner of her mouth lifted. "I owe you an apology," she replied.

I blinked. "What for?"

"For assuming," she said. "When Tristan told me about the prophecy, and then when you opened the box, I guess I thought you would complicate the plans I had to have Thomas and Tristan travel back to Europe with the Valentine relics." Her words hit like a dropped glass.

"Prophecy?" I repeated.

Her fingers stilled. Slowly, she looked up at me.

"He hasn't told you?" she asked.

My mouth felt dry. "Told me what?"

She took a step back but looked at me with her head tilted.

"Tristan has visions," she said carefully. "He always has. That's why the Order took him in as a child."

I couldn't hold her gaze, instead staring to stare at my own reflection in the mirror.

"And me?" I asked.

Seraphine hesitated. Just long enough.

"You were one of those visions," she said. "Lofn told him someone was coming. Someone that Tristan and Thomas would find love with."

Anger boiled in my gut.

"So, I was what," I said quietly. "A delivery?"

Her hand lifted, facing me palm up like she was trying to soothe a wild animal.

"No," she said at once. "That isn't how it was meant."

"But it *was* known," I said.

"And did you also say they were going to Europe?"

Seraphine straightened, visibly pulling herself back into composure. "I'm sorry," she said. "I assumed you knew."

"When?"

"I'm not sure it's my place. I wouldn't have spoken so freely if I'd realized—"

"It's fine," I cut in, too quickly.

Because if I didn't say it, I might say something else. Something sharp. Something I couldn't take back.

She nodded once. "I overstepped."

Footsteps sounded in the hall. Familiar voices. Tristan laughing at something Thomas said. I felt it then—the instinct I knew too well. The one that always came when things started to matter.

Push it down.

Pack it away.

I smiled, adjusted the fall of my dress, and turned just as the boys reached the door bright-eyed, warm, utterly unaware.

And I decided, very clearly, not to tell them any of this.

If they could keep things from me, then I could keep things from them.

It felt petty. It also felt like the only solid ground left.

The wedding blurred.

Daisy was radiant. Jack cried. Iris squeezed my hand during the vows, her eyes shining. I smiled when I was supposed to. Laughed at the right moments. Drank when someone put a drink in my hand.

But it was like watching it all through glass.

My head ached. My chest felt tight. Every time I laughed, it took effort to draw the next breath.

When the moon rose, my phone buzzed. And I knew it was time.

I stood, smoothed my dress, and followed the boys out into the night carrying my silence with me like armor.

CHAPTER 15

February 14
TRISTAN

The gardens were quieter beyond the marquee. String music, laughter and the clink of glasses spilled out in softened waves. But out here the night pressed closer, damp grass dark underfoot, fairy lights strung between trees like borrowed stars.

Thomas stopped near the edge of the lawn and set the Lofn Wedding Game puzzle box down on a stone bench. He'd brought it with him, tucked under his arm like something fragile and dangerous.

Poppy stood opposite us, her heels sinking slightly into the grass. The silk of her dress clung to her waist and my hand itched to touch her, but she'd kept herself out of arms reach for most of the event. She looked stunning—bare shoulders, hair swept up, the faint flush of wine and exhaustion in her cheeks.

"Is this going to work?" she asked. "If we do it here?"

Thomas nodded. "As long as we can see the moon, it's

perfect."

We all looked up at the new moon sitting high above us, then formed a loose triangle again. We no longer needed to stand as close, the distance between us wider now that the first and second trial had stretched the radius. But my body had already learned to crave her closeness.

Thomas exhaled slowly. He didn't look at either of us at first. His gaze dropped to his hand, to the ring circling his finger: bronze dulled by days of wear, etched marks catching the moonlight.

"You both remember what to say?" he asked quietly. And I saw Poppy nodding along with me. Having already said them twice before, I feel like the words had been scratched into my brain with a rusty nail. Thomas lifted his head then and looked between us.

"Once we say these words," he said, "we should be free." His voice was gruff, on the last word especially.

My throat tightened too. I nodded because there was nothing else to do. Because I couldn't find a version of myself that asked for more time without sounding selfish.

Poppy nodded too, short and sharp, her jaw set.

Thomas squared his shoulders. Locked himself into place.

"Under new moon's rebirth—"

The moment he began, and something in the air tightened in anticipation.

My mouth felt dry when I joined him. My chest

ached before the words even reached my tongue, like my body knew what my mind was trying to do and was revolting.

"—I, Tristan Roswell, reject this bond and revoke this vow."

Saying *reject* felt like driving my own hand into my ribs. The word scraped on the way out, pulled something loose behind my sternum.

Poppy said it last.

When she did, the magic hit. A violent release —like a cord drawn tight between the three of us had been cut without warning. The recoil slammed through me, sharp and sudden, stealing my breath. My knees nearly buckled as the pull vanished, leaving my body pitching forward into nothing.

Pain flared, bright and disorienting, then vanished just as fast, leaving a hollow in its wake. A stunned emptiness. My balance shifted. My awareness recalibrated.

The absence was immediate. Startling. Like losing a sense I hadn't known I possessed until it was gone.

Poppy didn't wait.

She yanked the ring off her finger and threw it down between us.

It struck the stone path with a hard metallic clink and spun once before settling.

"It worked," she spat.

My chest tightened. Not with the magic, but with the way she looked at us.

Thomas stared at the ring.

"It's what you wanted, isn't it?" she went on. Her voice shook, but it didn't break. "Now you can both go take your little Valentine show on the road."

She laughed then. A sharp, brittle sound. "Were you even going to even bother telling me you were leaving?"

My stomach dropped, and from the corner of my eye I saw Thomas flinch too.

"Poppy," I said, stepping toward her. "Please—"

She backed away, eyes flashing. "Don't."

"And the visions," she added, turning her gaze on me. "Your *prophecy*."

She said the last word with a vicious sneer that hit like a slap.

"Seraphine told you," I whispered.

"By mistake, yeah!" she shot back. "Which feels about right, actually. This whole damn thing has just been one big mistake from the second I agreed to take the stupid job."

She looked between us, something wounded and furious tightening her mouth.

"I was just some prize," she yelled. "Some sort of fucked up retention bonus or loyalty reward."

I opened my mouth. Nothing came out.

"Do you have any idea what that feels like?" she demanded. "To realize you weren't chosen—just *scheduled*?"

"That's not what it was," I said hoarsely. "Not for me. Not for us."

"It doesn't matter," she said dragging in a breath, like she was steadying herself against something internal and violent. "Because now the rings are gone. Whatever we felt," her voice was lower now, almost hissing the words at us, "it came with the game. It's gone now without it."

My heart kicked hard.

"That doesn't make it fake," I said. "My feelings are real."

She flinched. Just once.

"But mine aren't anymore." she replied.

That was the blow I couldn't block.

She looked past us then, toward the marquee, toward the light and music spilling out onto the lawn.

"So, you're free," she said. "Go. Take the offer. Chase the next thing. I don't want to see either of you again."

The music swelled behind us as the marquee doors opened. Light spilled across the lawn.

Daisy appeared first, white skirts gathered in her hands. Her wedding dress was simple and luminous, ivory silk, long sleeves, a low back dusted with lace. Iris was right behind her, sharp-eyed and already assessing the scene.

"Pop?" Daisy said softly.

Poppy swayed on her heels, hands flying out to find her balance. Thomas and I both started towards her, but Iris was there first, slipping an arm around her waist. Daisy took her other side.

"We've got her," Iris said to us, not unkindly— but final.

Jack and Sam hovered just behind them. Jack's jaw tightened as he took in Poppy's pale face. Sam's eyes flicked to me, then Thomas, and stayed there a second too long. Neither of them spoke. They didn't need to.

Poppy didn't look back as they guided her toward the marquee, back into the warm chaos of family and music and people who knew her history by heart.

Out of habit, I took one step after her, to maintain the radius distance before the pain of the binding could kick in. Only remembering after the door slammed shut behind them that the distance didn't hurt.

Then why is my heart still aching?

Thomas leaned down to pick up Poppy's ring, and put it in the puzzle box. He added his own and then put his hand out for mine too. I looked down at it and for a minute considered keeping it on.

"She's made her choice, Tristan."

I shut my eyes, and still saw her face. *Whatever we felt. It came with the game. It's gone now without it.*

Finally, I pulled off the ring and placed it in the box along with the other two. Thomas closed the box and stood very still, the sound of the latch final as a coffin lid.

The fairy lights buzzed faintly overhead. Somewhere inside, someone cheered. Glasses clinked. A new song started.

CHAPTER 16

February 17
POPPY

Three days later, and it should have felt like a clean break. I'd been through plenty of break-ups in my life, and I kept telling myself, this one would be no different.

Except, there I was, and it still felt like a bruise I kept pressing, just to prove it still hurt.

I lay on my side with my knees tucked up, staring at the thin slice of daylight between my blinds. The room smelled faintly of stale perfume and musty clothes. I'd thrown my bag from my time with the boys in the corner days ago and never moved it.

In the living room, I could hear Iris and Merry whisper-arguing about me through the door.

"She needs to eat," Merry hissed. "Or drink. Or blink. Literally anything besides this sad Victorian fainting-couch nonsense."

"It's not nonsense," Iris said.

"I know," Merry softened, just a fraction. "I know. I'm sorry. I just... I hate seeing her like this."

The couch creaked. A cup clinked against a coaster. Iris was probably making tea she wouldn't drink.

"She told us to give her space," Iris said.

Merry blew out a breath. "Yeah, space is the last thing that girl needs."

I squeezed my eyes shut.

The problem with being loved by women like Iris and Merry and even Daisy (who would probably be here too if she wasn't already on her honeymoon) was that they loved you out loud. They loved you in lists and plans and solutions. They loved you with food and phone chargers and blankets tucked around your feet. They loved you by refusing to let you disappear.

Right now, I wanted to be a ghost.

My chest ached in a way I told myself was heartbreak. A dull, stubborn pressure behind my ribs, like I'd swallowed a stone, and it was lodged there, refusing to go down.

Every time I shifted, something in my lungs crackled. I ignored it. I told myself it was nothing. Residue. Magic. Grief.

I dragged the duvet higher and rolled onto my back.

The ceiling fan was off, but I could still hear it in my head. A soft whirring that wasn't real.

My phone buzzed once on the bedside table. But I didn't reach for it. If it was Daisy, I couldn't handle her worry, and if it was them... I couldn't handle to even finish that thought either.

I stared at the ceiling until my eyes burned, then

I let them close.

Sleep came fast.

❋ ❋ ❋

When I woke, the room was darker. Evening light, bruised purple at the edges.

My throat felt raw. My tongue felt too big. My skin was hot and prickly.

I pushed myself upright and immediately had to stop and catch my breath. It shouldn't have been hard to breathe. The air felt thick, like I was pulling it through fabric.

I coughed once, sharp and wet, and my ribs lit up with pain.

My eyes watered. My nose ran.

I swung my legs over the side of the bed and stood, steadying myself with a hand on the dresser. The room tilted. Not spinning, just... not quite attached to me.

I took one step toward the door and the tightness in my chest deepened. I pressed a hand over my sternum, trying to flatten it away.

"Pop?" Iris's voice, at the door followed by a knock. "Can I come in?"

I didn't answer fast enough.

The door opened.

Iris stood there with a bowl of soup, her hair pulled into a messy bun. Her expression shifted from worry to alarm as soon as she saw me.

"Poppy," she gasped. "Sit down!"

"I'm fine," I tried. My voice came out thin.

I coughed again, and it took too much out of me. My knees wobbled.

Iris put the bowl down on my dresser and made her way to me swiftly, her hand raising to press the back to my forehead.

"You're burning up," she said.

"I'm just tired."

"Pop."

"What?" I asked, even though my mouth already felt too dry.

"Why didn't you tell me you were sick?"

"I'm not sick." Even as I said it, I could hear how stupid it sounded. My lungs were making a faint whistling sound like a kettle that didn't want to boil.

Iris grabbed my hand. "Shoes. Now."

"Iris, I don't need—"

"Yes, you do." She'd put on her big sister voice, so I knew I was in trouble. "Merry!"

Merry's footsteps pounded down the hall. "What is it?"

"She's sick," Iris said. "We're going to the hospital."

Merry's face went sharp. Focused. Useful. "Okay. I'll get my keys. Poppy where's your purse and I'll grab that too."

I tried to argue again, but instead fell into a fit of coughing.

Merry's eyes widened. "Okay, cool, I hate the

sound of that."

I put on my shoes and let Iris lead me out of the room, her arm tight around my waist, steering me like I was something fragile. Merry grabbed my coat and wrapped it around me. The cold hallway air outside my apartment door hit my fever skin and made me shiver so hard my teeth clicked. And then the world slid sideways into headlights and streetlights and Iris's voice soothing my name as she brushed my hair from my face.

✽ ✽ ✽

Hospital light is different from every other kind of light.

It's too bright. Too clean. It makes me feel like a specimen under a microscope, exposed and see-through.

They put me in a room with one bed and one chair that folded out into a something. Iris paced. Merry sat on the edge of the chair like she was ready to launch herself at a doctor if they took too long.

A nurse clipped something to my finger. Another wrapped a cuff around my arm. Someone asked me to rate my pain. I wanted to tell them it wasn't the kind of pain with a number.

A doctor came in with tired eyes and a brisk voice.

"Poppy Everly?" he said.

I nodded. It took effort.

"You've got pneumonia," he said, like he was naming an inconvenience. Then he looked at my chart again and his mouth tightened. "Your oxygen saturation is low, and your fever is very high. With stats like this I imagine you've been unwell for a while. You should have come in much sooner."

Iris made a small sound. A sharp inhale. And I could hear Merry's teeth grind as her jaw clenched.

My head just ran with images of a storm in the woods. Rain soaking through my clothes. Running until my lungs burned. Standing there screaming.

I swallowed. It scraped.

The doctor continued "You're going to be okay. We're going to start IV fluid and antibiotics and give you some oxygen. But you need to stop fighting your own body, and get some rest."

I wanted to tell him I wasn't fighting my body. I was fighting my heart. Instead, I closed my eyes and let the nurse fit the oxygen prongs under my nose. Cool air slid into me.

It should have been comforting.

It felt like surrender.

* * *

I drifted.

Voices came and went. Machines beeped in gentle rhythms. My skin alternated between clammy and too hot. Somewhere in the middle of the night, I woke up coughing so hard my ribs screamed. Iris pressed the call button with shaking fingers. A nurse adjusted something, murmured reassurance, told me to breathe slow.

Sleep dragged me under again.

This time, it wasn't sleep.

It was a room that wasn't my room.

The hospital walls faded into something darker, warmer. Candlelight, maybe. Or just the glow of something old.

The air smelled like smoke and cedar and rain on stone.

Someone sat at the foot of my bed.

Not a doctor.

Not Iris.

Not Merry.

A woman, long-legged and relaxed, like she had all the time in the world. Denim clung to her thighs, but above it she wore a white peasant top with flowy sleeves that shimmered when she shifted. Her hair was braided, copper wire threaded through it, catching the low light. The kind of beauty that didn't ask to be admired. It demanded it.

"Poor little flame," she murmured.

My mouth wouldn't work. My body wouldn't move. I could only stare. Her eyes flicked to my hand. To the place where the ring had been and I could somehow feel her eyes looking for it. She leaned forward, resting her elbows on her knee, chin in her hand.

"You think you were tricked," she said. "You think you were taken."

I tried to shake my head. I don't know if I did.

"You think love is a snare. Something that tightens until you cannot breathe." Her voice held no mockery. Only the air of one telling a child, they're not angry, just disappointed.

My throat burned. My chest hurt. I wanted to tell her she didn't understand.

She smiled, and it was the smile of someone who'd watched humans make the same mistake for centuries.

"I did not bind you to shrink you," she said. "I bound you to make you look. To keep you still long enough to see the thing that could save you."

Save me?

Her hand lifted, fingers flicking, like she was brushing lint off the air. "They had their own cages," she went on. "Duty. Insecurity. Ambition. They worshiped sacrifice so hard they forgot they were allowed to want."

Her eyes sharpened on me. "And you, Poppy Everly."

My skin prickled at my name on her tongue.

"You were so afraid of becoming small that you chose to disappear from love all together."

Heat rose behind my eyes. I couldn't cry. I couldn't breathe right. I could only feel the truth of it settle in my gut, heavy and ugly.

She stood. The room shifted with her. Like the world remembered she was in charge.

"Cowardice is not a mortal sin," she said. "It is simply a habit."

She stepped closer and placed her fingers lightly on my forehead. Cool. Then warm. Then something like sunlight under my skin.

"Enough," she murmured. The fever inside me shuddered, and began to dissolve away.

"Choose," she whispered, and her voice softened on the last word, almost gentle. "When you can."

Then she was gone. The room snapped back into fluorescent light and beeped machines and oxygen air.

I gasped. And for the first time in days, I drew a breath that didn't feel like drowning.

*　*　*

When I woke properly, it was morning.

The curtains were half open. Grey daylight. Iris dozing in the chair, head tilted back, mouth slightly open. Her hand was still curled around the edge of the blanket on my bed, like she'd refused to let go even in sleep.

My body felt wrecked. But the fever had eased. My thoughts, for the first time, weren't swimming.

A nurse came in and checked my vitals, murmuring approval. Iris woke and blinked at me.

"You're better," she said, voice thick.

"Don't say it like you're surprised," I tried. My

voice was still rough, but it worked.

Iris laughed weakly, tears rising fast. "I was so worried about you."

I didn't have the strength to comfort her the way she deserved. I only squeezed her fingers.

Later, after Iris had left, my parents arrived.

My father wore a tidy sweater and had a newspaper tucked under his arm. My mother wore a tailored coat that probably cost more than my rent and held herself like the hospital was an inconvenience she could out-posture.

And yet, when she saw me, her face did something strange.

It softened.

Just for a second. Like the mask slipped.

She came to the bedside, touching my arm with careful fingers, as if she wasn't used to tenderness anymore.

"You scared us," she said.

My father gave me a short nod, before taking the seat Iris offered.

"I'm okay," I said, and meant it, physically even though my heart still felt far from okay.

My mother sat on the edge of the bed, crossing her legs, smoothing her skirt. I looked at her hands and the giant diamond ring on her left, glinting in the hospital fluorescence. Then I looked at my hands. Bare fingers. No rings. Nothing to prove what had happened.

I stared at her, and the memory hit me like a flash of home video.

A woman on a tennis court. Laughing. Loud. Hair pulled back, sun on her shoulders. A wicked serve. A grin that took up space.

A wild free woman, not the woman who critiqued table settings and wedding guest lists. Not the woman who measured everything I did against what she called "appropriate."

I swallowed. My chest tugged with a different kind of pain.

"Mom," I said quietly. Looking over at my father already absorbed in the finance section of his paper.

She looked up, wary, like she expected a complaint.

"Did you ever regret it?" The words came out before I could sand them down. "Giving up... all of it."

Her eyes narrowed. "All what dear?"

"Your tennis career?" My throat tightened. "Do you regret stepping away from it all, for us? To have a family and all that."

For a moment, my mother's expression froze.

Then her gaze slid away, to my father in the chair, with his nose in the newspaper. When she spoke, her voice was lower than I'd ever heard it.

"I didn't give up tennis for the family," she said. "I was injured."

I blinked. "What? I saw the old videos, saw the timestamp. It all seemed to line up. Your last tournament was only the year before Iris was born."

"Well yes. That's true. But after that tournament I was having excruciating pain up my arm. It was a stress fracture," she said briskly, like naming it made it smaller. "The third in two years. My father wanted me to keep playing through the pain. But I was done. I had met your father, and already discovered I didn't need tennis to feel remarkable, to feel valued. Your father's love made me feel that way. Then later, I found having my girls made me feel that way."

My lungs pulled in a careful breath.

"I thought…" My voice cracked. "I thought you chose love over your career."

My mother's gaze snapped back to mine, sharp.

"I chose to stop letting my father live through my body," she said, and there was steel in it. "Choosing your father, was a choice for myself."

I stared at her, stunned.

She inhaled. Exhaled. The softness flickered again. Then her chin lifted, and it was gone.

My throat burned. My eyes stung. I didn't know what to do with this. I'd seen those videos of my mother during my freshman year at college. All my adult life, I'd been afraid of love because I thought it came with an eraser. That it rubbed you down until you were easier to keep.

And now my mother was telling me… that I was wrong. That I'd made a huge mistake.

My chest ached, not with fever now, but with regret. Because I had seen two men look at me like I was a sunrise. And I had called it fake.

My mother stood abruptly, smoothing her coat again like she could press the emotion back into place.

"I'm going to find a nurse," she said. "They never

check on you when they should."

But as she turned, her hand brushed my father's shoulder. Gentle. Habitual. Real.

When she left, the room felt too quiet. I stared at the date on the little whiteboard near the door.

February 20.

My throat tightened.

They were leaving soon. Early March. That was what Seraphine had said. They had wanted it. They had worked for it. And I had told them to go.

I closed my eyes.

Cowardice is simply a habit.

I didn't know if I could break it fast enough. My chest rose, slow and careful, the oxygen helping. My body was healing. My heart was behind, limping.

In the quiet, I admitted the thing I hadn't let myself say since the woods.

I loved them.

Not the rings. Not the prophecy. Not the heat of a storm.

Them.

And it was too late. I lay there listening to my father breathe in the chair, listening to my own lungs struggle toward strength, and felt the full weight of what I'd done settle over me.

CHAPTER 17

February 20
THOMAS

I packed books because it gave my hands something to do. If I stopped, I'd have to think about her. And if I thought about her, I wouldn't be able to keep pretending this departure made sense.

I stacked them carefully on the desk—spines aligned, weight balanced—small, precise decisions that didn't ask anything of me beyond order.

A slim volume on comparative ritual law. A binder of donor briefs. A hardback on medieval relic authentication. Anything that made my hands look busy and my mind look useful. Anything that wasn't the obvious.

Anything that wasn't the thought of her.

The library smelled like old paper and cedar polish, the kind of quiet that usually suited me. Tonight, it pressed in. The hearth was lit, and the fire made the spines of the books glow like they were still alive.

Across the room, Tristan sat on the couch with a book open on his lap. He hadn't turned a page in ten minutes.

He stared through the paper, thumb tapping the edge. Every so often he checked his phone, then set it down again with a slow, careful movement, like he didn't trust himself not to throw it.

Since Valentine's night, he'd been... contained. I should have said something. A thousand things.

Instead, I kept packing.

Because if I stopped, if I let my mind do what it wanted, I'd be out the front door and, in my car, and halfway to her apartment before I could even say 'medieval relic authentication'. I'd be on her doorstep, palms up, begging her to forgive us. Telling her I didn't know how to live without the tether my body had learned as *home*.

But instead of doing that, I slipped another book into the pile on the desk and tried not to think about how the room felt too large now. How the air didn't have her in it. How the manor didn't sound right without her laughter bouncing off the ceilings.

My thoughts were gratefully interrupted when my laptop chimed.

A call request popped up. *Unknown number.*

Tristan's head snapped up.

The movement was so fast it almost startled me.

"Probably a vendor," I said, already reaching for the trackpad.

It was late. Seraphine wouldn't be calling me on

an unknown number. The Order wouldn't either. We were leaving soon. There were a hundred loose ends, and none of them mattered more than getting out of this building before I did something reckless.

I clicked decline.

The browser window opened anyway.

For a moment I thought I'd mis-clicked, that I'd accepted it by accident, but the screen filled with a woman's face and the soft blur of a familiar space behind her. A half-visible kitchen. A couch with a throw blanket tossed over one end. A little shelf crowded with puzzle boxes.

My lungs forgot what they were for. I knew that apartment.

The woman on-screen leaned closer, bright-eyed, hair pulled back in a haphazard scrunchy.

"Hi," she said briskly. "Okay. Good. It worked."

Tristan was on his feet before she'd finished the sentence, crossing the room in three strides. "Who are you?"

Her mouth quirked. "Merry."

The name meant nothing to me. Not at first.

Then I remembered a laugh at the bachelorette party call. A voice in the background, warm and bossy and amused.

Tristan hovered behind my shoulder, close enough that I could feel his heat. His eyes were too sharp. Too hungry.

Merry glanced between us and her eyes softened with obvious pity.

"How did you get this number?" I asked, my

question coming out colder than intended.

Merry didn't flinch. "Yeah, well. I'm a problem-solver. You were hard to track down. But your privacy settings are medieval. Have you never heard of multi-factor authentication?"

I stared at the background again, my throat tightening at the sight of Poppy's puzzle shelf, her kitchen counter, the space where I had watched her trip through discarded piles of laundry to find a pair of shoes she had to pack.

"Where is she?" I asked.

Merry's expression shifted. Just a flicker. A small seriousness settling in like a weight.

"She's in hospital," she said. "With pneumonia."

The word hit like a blunt object.

Tristan made a sound, barely audible. Something ripped from deep in his chest.

"Is she—" he started, then stopped. His voice broke on the edge of the question.

Merry's gaze softened. "She's being treated. But she's really sick."

"Pneumonia," I echoed. It was all I could manage with the barrage of screaming terrors pummelling my brain.

Merry shrugged, but it wasn't casual. "She got worse over the last few days. Iris thought at first it was just the... breakup." She stammered on the last word, clearly unsure if it was the right word for what Poppy, Tristan and I had been through. "Anyway, she was sleeping a lot. Not eating. Then she started wheezing, and her fever spiked bad. Iris freaked out and took her to the hospital."

I forced my hand to unclench from the edge of the desk. I hadn't realized I'd grabbed it.

"Why are you calling?" Tristan asked. His voice was steadier now, which meant it was barely being held together.

Merry lifted her chin. "Because you two were... magically attached to her. So, I thought I'd check if this was maybe all some kind of supernatural side-effect?"

I blinked.

A logical thread. Something I could follow.

"We're fine," I said, too quickly. "Magic didn't cause this." But even as I said the words, I wondered if they were true. Hadn't it been the magic that had put us out in the middle of the woods on a stormy winter night? Where else might she have caught pneumonia?

Merry's mouth tightened, sympathy and impatience at war. "Okay. Well. If it's not magic-induced, then great, it shouldn't need a magic cure or anything. The doctors should have it handled."

"Where is she?" I asked again, sharper now. "Which hospital?"

Merry leaned forward, and the camera angle shifted. For a second, I saw the side of Poppy's couch, the outline of a blanket, and my chest did something ugly at the thought of her lying there alone.

"She's at St. Vincent's," Merry said. "Private room. I can send the number to this email." She glanced down, fingers moving quickly, the sound of typing faint through the speakers. "Done."

Tristan's hand landed on my shoulder, firm.

Merry watched us, eyes sharp.

"If you're going to do something, do it now. If you're not... don't. She's already broken."

I didn't give her an answer.

I didn't trust my voice.

I reached for the mouse, ended the call, and stood so fast the chair scraped loudly across the floor. Tristan was already moving, grabbing his coat off the back of the couch.

We didn't speak.

We didn't need to.

We burst into the corridor like the manor itself was trying to hold us back. The lights were dimmed for the evening, gilded frames staring down, centuries of saints and lovers and martyrs watching us run like idiots.

We rounded the corner and almost collided with Seraphine.

She was coming from the direction of her suite, tablet in hand, hair pinned neatly, every inch of her arranged control. But she stopped at the sight of us, eyes narrowing.

"Thomas?" she said. "Tristan? What is—"

"She's in hospital," Tristan blurted.

Seraphine's mouth tightened. "Who?"

The fact that she had to ask made something hot and bitter flare behind my ribs.

"Poppy," I said, and the name came out like a vow of its own.

Seraphine's gaze flicked to my face, then Tristan's, and something in her expression recalibrated. Not alarm. Not anger.

Assessment.

"Hospital," she repeated, and it was a question now. "Why?"

"Pneumonia," I said.

Seraphine's brows drew together. "She's been ill?"

"Because she ran into a storm for us," Tristan snapped, then immediately swallowed the sharpness. "Because we dragged her into this. Because—"

Because we loved her. Because she'd been ours. Because we'd let her go.

Seraphine looked between us again, and now the pragmatic gears started turning.

"The flight—" she said, as if reminding us.

"We can't go," I said.

Tristan turned to me. Surprise, then relief, then a flare of something raw and grateful.

Seraphine stilled. "Thomas."

"We can't go," I repeated. "Not now."

Seraphine's voice sharpened, not unkindly. "You're reacting emotionally. This is a significant opportunity. It is not easily offered twice."

I laughed once, short and humorless. "You think I don't know that?"

Her eyes narrowed further. "Then explain."

Tristan spoke, softer. "We have to see her."

Seraphine's gaze shifted to him, then back to me. "Because you feel responsible?"

No.

Because I want her. Because I can't breathe

without her. Because the thought of her alone in a hospital bed makes something savage rise in me and I don't know where to put it.

Seraphine's tone was careful now. "I assumed the bond was the only source of the attachment."

Her eyes held mine when she said it.

As if she'd been watching me, waiting, not quite believing I was capable of this kind of reckless devotion. As if she'd thought I was all ambition and discipline and steel.

The irony almost made me choke.

"The bond was a tether," I said, voice low. "It wasn't the reason."

Tristan's breath caught beside me.

Seraphine's lips parted slightly, then pressed back together. "Thomas—"

"I love her," I said.

The hallway went very quiet.

It didn't feel dramatic when it left my mouth. It felt like truth finally allowed to exist in the open air. Like a confession and a weapon and a promise all at once.

Tristan made a strangled sound, half laugh, half pain, and I knew he'd been waiting for me to say it.

Seraphine's face shifted. Not surprise. Something closer to... recalibration. As if she'd made a calculation years ago and was now realizing the numbers had changed.

"I love her," I said again, because I wanted no room for misunderstanding. "We both love her. And if she dies while we're on a plane to impress donors and perform demonstrations, then none of it matters. None of it."

Seraphine's jaw tightened. "She is not dying from pneumonia."

"You don't know that," I argued, even as I willed it to be true. My voice stayed controlled, but I could feel it. The crack in the shell. The pressure behind my eyes. The sheer violence of the thought.

Tristan stepped closer. "Seraphine. Please."

She looked at us both.

Then, finally, she exhaled.

"Consequences," she said. "If you do this, you may lose the trip. You may lose standing. You may lose —"

"I know," I said.

"Thomas, your promotion—"

"I know."

Tristan's hand found mine for a second, a brief grip. Solidarity. Brotherhood.

Seraphine held our gaze, and for the first time in days, I saw something like softness in her. Not sentimentality. Understanding.

"I will handle it." she said briskly, already shifting into action.

Tristan blinked. "You're... letting us go?"

"I'm not your mother," she said dryly. Then, quieter, almost to herself: "And if I was, I would not be interested in raising men who can recite the Order's mission but cannot live it."

The words landed harder than any reprimand.

I didn't thank her. There wasn't time. The

manor tried to swallow us as we ran. The long corridors. The grand staircase. The polished floors that made our footsteps too loud.

Outside, the cold bit immediately.

The car was in the drive. My hands shook as I unlocked it.

Tristan got in, seatbelt snapping into place like he needed the restraint. His phone was already in his hand, scrolling through Merry's message again and again like it might change.

I started the engine.

The tyres spat gravel as I pulled out.

We drove fast. We drove like men who had spent their whole lives believing control was the only way to survive, and who had finally met something they couldn't control at all.

The road blurred under the headlights. The trees were black ribs against the sky.

Every worst-case scenario lined up in my mind like soldiers.

Her skin too pale.

Her eyes closed.

Machines beeping. Machines no longer beeping.

I drove faster.

"Thomas," Tristan said once, voice tight. Not a warning. A plea.

I didn't answer. Because if I spoke, I might admit the fear aloud, and then it would become real in a way I couldn't contain.

The city lights appeared, smeared gold through the windscreen. The hospital rose ahead, bright and sterile and too far away. I swung into the parking structure, barely finding a spot, barely cutting the engine before we were out, slamming doors, running.

Merry's text sat on Tristan's screen: room number, wing, floor.

We bolted through automatic doors. Harsh fluorescent light washed over us. The smell hit: disinfectant, warm plastic, something faintly human and afraid.

A nurse called after us. We didn't stop.

We took stairs because the elevator took too long.

Two steps at a time.

Three.

My lungs burned. My heart pounded like it was trying to beat its way out of my ribs.

We hit the corridor and turned, following the signs, following the number.

The door was ahead.

Tristan reached it first, hand hovering over the handle like he didn't know if he was allowed.

I caught up beside him, chest heaving, fingers curling into a fist.

All the ambition. All the planning. All the careful control.

None of it mattered.

Only this did.

Together we pushed the door open.

CHAPTER 18

February 20
TRISTAN

Poppy was sitting up in the hospital bed, pillows stacked behind her, a thin tube looped beneath her nose, a line taped to her arm. She looked pale. Smaller than she had any right to be. But she was sitting upright, and her eyes were bright and sharp as they always were.

For a second, the room tilted.

Not from any magic this time. It was just pure unadulterated relief washing through me and soothing all the frayed and tormented edges that had ripped open in my chest since we got the news about her illness. Thomas stopped beside me, close enough that I could feel the way he trembled too. I didn't look at him. I couldn't take my eyes from her. But I reached out and clenched his hand, squeezing it tight to help ground us both in the reality that she was ok.

She blinked at us like she didn't quite believe we were real either.

"Hi?" she said it like a question, and I hated that

there could be any doubt in her mind that we would be here for her.

"We came as fast as we could," I said, the words tumbling out rough and unpractised. "Merry called. She told us you were sick and—" I swallowed. "We're sorry we didn't know sooner."

Her gaze flicked between us, wary now. Guarded.

"You didn't have to come," she said.

"Yes," Thomas said quietly. "We did." There was a rough quality to his words, and I noticed he had yet to release my hand.

She waved a hand like she was brushing off her situation as overly dramatic, but I saw her wince as she shifted on the bed.

I let go of Thomas and stepped closer. My brain unhelpfully recalled how this was exactly the distance we were previously bound to when we first slipped on the rings. But while there was no more pull or pain outside this radius, the ache of wanting her had not dissipated in the least.

"I owe you the truth," I said. "All of it."

Her jaw tightened.

"I should have told you about my visions," I continued. "About Lofn. About what she said. Not because the prophecy mattered, but because you matter. I was afraid if I told you I would be taking the choice from you. And I—" Thomas had stepped forward now too, his hand moving to rest on my shoulder, "And we... We wanted you to choose us on your own."

She looked down at her hands, her fingers fidgeting where Lofn's ring had previously been.

"I didn't tell you how I felt either," I said. "And that's on me. I've spent my whole life being grateful for what I was given, careful not to ask for more. But the first moment you crashed into me on that rooftop, I wanted you."

Silence stretched, heavy and breathing.

Thomas cleared his throat, like he needed the moment to hold.

"I love you," he said.

He didn't soften it. Didn't qualify it. And I heard Poppy's breath hitch as they landed.

"I told myself it was the bond," he continued. "That it was chemistry, proximity—something explainable." His jaw tightened, and even the fingers he had resting on my shoulder seemed to clench. "But every version of the future that didn't include you felt... wrong. Hollow."

He looked at her then, fully.

"Walking away without choosing you scared me more than losing everything I've worked for."

I watched her face as it shifted, the walls cracking, the fear underneath surfacing.

"You were always free," I said softly. "We never wanted you because you were promised. We wanted you because you were you."

She pressed her palms to her face for a long moment, hiding whatever emotion my words had elicited.

"I thought it was all fake," she whispered into

her palms. Then she looked up and continued, "The feelings. I thought I was just... convenient. A problem to solve."

"No," I said fiercely. But before I could tell her how wrong this was, she put her hand up to stop me.

"Please, let me get this out." Her hand returned to her lap, and she took a deep steadying breath. "I was so scared," she said. "Of shrinking. Of waking up one day and realizing I'd traded myself away."

"You didn't," Thomas said. "And you never will. Not for us. Not for anyone."

Her eyes filled, and this time she didn't blink it back.

"I love you both too," she said, the tears spilling onto her cheeks.

The words hit me like oxygen.

Like surfacing.

I didn't remember moving, only that my hands found hers, warm and real, and my lips pressed a kiss to her knuckles.

"We love you," I said, looking deep into those sharp green eyes. "Every day. Every way."

Thomas leaned in then, careful, reverent, brushing a kiss to her hair, and wiping the tears from her face with his thumb.

A nurse cleared her throat pointedly from the doorway.

We chuckled softly and stepped back, my hands still tangled with hers, Thomas's resting on her shoulder. There was no magic tethering us anymore, and yet none of us were unwilling to let go.

CHAPTER 19

February 23
THOMAS

The discharge papers were still folded in my pocket. The doctor had said *rest, fluids, someone with her overnight.* We had all nodded, solemn and obedient.

Poppy had insisted on coming back to her apartment. Not the manor. Not yet.

I didn't argue. There would be time, I told myself. For conversations. For decisions. For us to shape this however we needed.

For now, I just wanted her somewhere she felt like herself.

Tristan and I walked her up the steps between us, matching her pace, pretending we weren't watching for any falter in her stride.

Her apartment was exactly as I remembered it, albeit maybe a bit tidier. The piles of laundry had been put away since we were last here and the air smelled faintly of citrus cleaner, sharp and clean beneath the softer layers of lived-in warmth. The windows were cracked open just enough to let the late-afternoon light spill in, catching on the edges of her mismatched furniture.

Tristan drifted ahead of me, carrying her overnight bag into the bedroom, while I stayed in the living room.

By the far window on a shelf nestled between a row of abstract-shaped puzzles sat the wooden box.

Lofn's Wedding Game.

The craftsmanship caught the light: intricately carved slots and latches, the wood grain dark and polished smooth. Seraphine had sent it to Poppy the day after we had told her about her illness, a note tucked beneath it in her precise hand.

For what you survived. And what you chose.

Seraphine had departed that morning, taking on the travel itinerary in our stead. And while she was gone, I would be acting Head of the chapter. It was a temporary promotion, and I enjoyed the work, but I found myself in no hurry to take on the position, or any like it, on a permanent basis.

Poppy's voice brought my attention from the box and the bedroom.

"I'm fine," she said huffing with frustration. "But I need a minute. Alone."

There was a pause.

"I can help—"

"No," she cut in, sharper than necessary. "You've helped enough. Please get out."

Tristan hesitated just long enough that I knew he was weighing whether to argue. Then he reappeared in the living room, brows drawn.

"She kicked me out," he said under his breath.

I lifted a shoulder. "Did she?"

"She's up to something," he said.

I trusted Tristan's intuition and tried not to worry about why she needed space already. It seemed, Lofn still trusted him too as his visions hadn't stopped either. Even though he had admitted to us he had feared they would now the trials were over. But just last night he'd told us that he'd been visited by her again, and a new couple was on the way to the Order. According to Lofn, they were still a few days away from arriving, so we still had plenty of time to connect with Poppy again now she was better.

So, we waited.

The apartment settled around us—pipes ticking faintly, the hum of the fridge, late-afternoon light stretching longer across the floor.

"Umm, can you both come in here please?" Poppy called out from behind the closed bedroom door. The uncertain edge in her voice set my pulse racing.

Tristan and I exchanged a glance and moved together down the short hall. I reached for the door first, my imagination supplying images of what could be on the other side. Poppy on the bed, pale and dizzy. Or worse.

I opened the door.

She was neither pale, nor apparently dizzy. But she was stretched across the bed, emerald lace decorating her otherwise bare skin, the color throwing her eyes into sharp, dangerous focus. Her hair was spilled loose around her shoulders, her cheeks flushed, and mouth curved in a smile that was all invitation and intent.

"Well?" she asked lightly, her gaze flicking between us. "Are you just going to stand there?"

Tristan swore softly beside me. Then immediately started slipping off his shirt. I was quick to follow his lead.

When we were both naked, we looked at each other, sharing a flash of conspiratorial excitement. I raised my eyebrow as if to say, 'shall we?' and Tristan responded with a grin before we both joined her on the bed.

We spent the first moments just kissing and touching and caressing. Reminding ourselves how it felt to be together again.

Tristan was on Poppy's left, propped on one elbow. And I took her righthand side, lifting her leg and hooking it over mine to expose her lace-clad pussy. Sandwiched between us, she kissed each of us in turn while three sets of hands stroked and caressed across lace and skin. My own fingers danced down Poppy's smooth stomach and across Tristan's hips.

If anyone tried asked me which of them I loved the most, I would have no answer.

How could I choose between these two people, who love me and each other? It was impossible. There was no Poppy without Tristan, and while Tristan had been my best friend for over a decade, the love we shared now could not have grown to what it is without Poppy.

There was no 'us' without every single one of the three.

While Tristan continued to rain kisses down onto Poppy's face and neck, I started kissing up her wrist, working my way up to her shoulders. My cock was achingly hard, and I pressed into the radiating warmth of her hip.

Eager to escalate from kissing, I slipped a slow hand down the front of her panties and began to stroke at the wetness. I found her clit and circled it with a slight pressure that caused her to a moan into Tristan's mouth. When she started bucking into my hand I withdrew, and she whimpered at the loss. With a grin I started to pull down her panties, while Tristan tugged down one of her bra straps. He slid his hand in to caress the liberated breast, before repeating the actions with the other. Together we worked to strip her completely of her lace lingerie, exposing her pretty pink pussy and pebbled nipples.

Fuck, she was a sight to behold.

Tristan began to suck hungrily at her left nipple, while I grabbed her other breast, and all the while she continued to stroke and tease us, her hands tracing close, but never quite touching our cocks. It was maddeningly arousing, hoping that every sweep of her hand would be the one to brush it, to grasp it, to give me some relief.

When it was clear she was intent on her tease, I decided to turn the table. And while Tristan stayed occupied with alternating his attention on her breasts, I shuffled down the bed to settle between her legs.

With my face inches from her centre, I was surprised when my eye caught on something sparkly.

"And what is this?" I growled, knowing full well what it was, but enjoying the way she squirmed at my question.

"It's um, I guess a bit of a warm-up."

I grabbed at her ass cheeks, pulling them to the side to get a better view of the green jeweled butt plug glistening in the light. I looked up at her and Tristan both so I could watch their faces as I asked:

"Does this mean you are greedy for both of us? At the same time?"

Even saying the words out loud seemed to turn her on, and as she threw her head back and moaned her reply.

"Oh god, yes. Yes please!"

Tristan seemed equally excited at the idea. I looked around her room, finding what I was after on her bedside table. I got up and grabbed the small bottle of lube before returning to my place between her legs.

I squirted some of the lube onto my finger, tossing the bottle onto the bed within reach, and circled one slippery finger around the jewel, teasing at the tight sensitive flesh it invaded.

With my other hand I used two fingers to rub her clit in matching slow circles. Poppy let out little mewls of pleasure and Tristan took the invitation of her exposed throat to kiss her neck and the sensitive spot beneath her ear.

Gliding the slickness of her pussy down, I added it to the lube and then pulled at the base of the jeweled plug. It resisted a little, but patiently I pushed and pulled at it, continuing my circles on her clit until she relaxed, and the plug pulled free.

The sight was so erotic, watching the muscles of her core and ass throb, I begun to grind my erection into the mattress. The friction helped my desire, but not nearly enough. I wanted to be inside this hot wet cunt more than I had wanted anything in my life.

Instead, I reached for the lube, squirting more back onto the plug, before tossing the bottle again and pressing two tick fingers into her pussy, and curling them against her g-spot. At the same time, I began to gently push the plug back into her anus. Gently, I pulsed it, pushing it in a little further each time, until the whole thing fit snugly back in. Poppy gasped, shifting her ass as the toy stretched her again.

"Oh, you took that so beautifully, my sweet Poppy." I praised, looking up to see Tristan watching with rapt delight at what I was doing. His own hands stroked at his rigid cock, pre-cum already beading at his tip, while Poppy clenched her fingers into the bedsheets.

I continued to pulse my fingers in and out of her pussy, the wet noises turned me on all the more, and I noticed myself grinding deeper into the mattress. Still stroking his cock, Tristan reached down and added one of the fingers from his other hand to mine inside her pussy. Our three fingers stretched her, both of us feeling her orgasm build as she clenched down on us.

I pulled at the plug again, and this time it slid out easier. I looked to Tristan and saw my desire matched on his face.

He turned to back to Poppy and asked, "Are you ready for us darling?"

"Please," she moaned.

"Please what?"

"Fuck me. Please. Both of you. Fuck me." She panted.

I stood up, tossing the plug on the bed by the lube and watched as Poppy and Tristan shuffled into position on the bed. While I waited, I stroked the residual wetness on my fingers from Poppy's pussy and the lube up and down my shaft, squeezing myself tight at the base and rolling back up to my head in long languid movements.

Tristan had moved to the edge of the bed, his feet planted on the floor. Poppy was straddling him her legs folded either side of him with her back to his chest, looking up at me standing over them.

"Lift up a bit" I instructed.

When she lifted her hips, I took Tristan's cock firmly in hand, holding it straight up and gliding the broad tip from her clit and down the cleft of her pussy, up and down a few times. Using his cock as a new toy to tease her with. I could hear both of their breaths get faster as I teased them both.

I reached for the lube bottle again, dribbling some onto his shaft and working it all over his length before I guided his cock to her rear entrance. I held Tristan's cock in place while he pulled apart the globes of her ass. Poppy took a deep shuddering breath as she lowered herself down. I released my grip on Tristan's thick cock, watching as it stretched her ass, opening her, filling her.

"Fuuuuck," Tristan groaned as she sank.

"Oh god," Poppy whimpered, burying her face in Tristan's neck.

"Is it too much?" I asked, and she shook her head in reply, eyes shut and mouth slack with the pleasure of it.

"Lean back against me," Tristan said. And as she reclined back, his hands went to her breasts, cupping them as his thumb flicked her nipples.

I continued to stroke my cock as I watched Tristan slowly guide her hips up and down a few times. I felt my cock swell in my hand as I watched Tristan's slick dick enter and withdraw from her ass, leaving her pussy open and glistening for me.

"Fuck, I need that pussy." I growled

I moved between their knees, tapping the tip of my cock against her swollen clit a few times. She gasped out, arching her back and pushing her tits harder into Tristan's hands, while hers clung desperately to the sheets at his sides.

The angle and Tristan's cock made it a tight fit, and I couldn't believe how good, how right, how utterly fucking divine she felt as I slid myself into her fully. I didn't move at first, just enjoyed the experience of truly being together. But soon the urge to move was overwhelming and I pulled back and started to move. Each of my thrusts lifted her off Tristan's cock, and when I pulled back, her body weight pushed her down on him once more. We continued to move like that, rocking and thrusting, the rhythm picking up and gathering steam.

Poppy came first, the orgasm clenching around us tight enough to slow our movements.

"I love you," she cried out even as her legs shook. "I love you both so much."

"We're yours," I roared pistoning my hips as I came as well, the orgasm blasting through me like a meteor shower. Blow after blow of fire-bright pleasure ricocheting through my body.

"Yours," Tristan agreed as he grabbed her hips and thrusted a few more times before he shuddered with his own climax.

✽ ✽ ✽

Later, tangled in sheets and warmth, I lay on my back with Poppy draped across my chest and Tristan's arm thrown over both of us. The city outside her window was beginning to pale, dawn thinning the dark. I had been awake for a while, listening to their breathing, content to stay still and let the moment last. Poppy stirred against me, a small sound leaving her throat as she shifted closer. My thumb traced slow, absent circles along her arm.

Her lashes fluttered, but they quickly settled closed again.

"Will you help me pack later?" she murmured,

voice rough with sleep.

I stilled.

"Will there be room for my stuff at the manor?" she asked, finally opening her eyes and lifting her head just enough to look at me. There was a sliver of fear in her eyes, like she was worried I might say 'no'. "I just want us to be all together. Close. If that's ok?"

I smiled down at her. And even though Tristan still slept, I knew I could answer for the both of us with absolute certainty.

"That would be more than ok. We'd love that," I said, pressing a kiss to her temple. The smile she beamed back was bright and wide.

"Take me home," she said, before sighing, content, and curling closer in my arms.

THE END

COMING SOON...

Merry will be back soon with her
own story in late 2026:

Christmas Charmed

To get updates on the release date and
any other news, follow me on
Instagram: @j_c_clayton

ABOUT THE AUTHOR

J C Clayton

Jacynta lives in Melbourne with her husband, two wild-hearted boys, and an ever-growing collection of books and crystals. A longtime professional content writer and editor, the Love & Lore novellas are her first published works of fiction  —and the beginning of a long-held dream finally coming true.

When she's not writing (or wrestling with what to write next), she's likely pulling tarot cards, soaking up live music, or adding to her collection of tattoos. She's a rebel at heart who believes in magic, mischief, and the power of a good happily-ever-after.